The Windsor Love Match

One bed. Two enemies. Cue the accidental cuddling.

Lizzie Chantree

lemon meringue

PUBLISHING

Cover image: Fitie, Popmarleo.
Cover design: Lizzie Chantree

 Formatted with Vellum

About this edition

The Windsor Love Match is written and edited in British English rather than American English. This includes spelling, grammar and punctuation.

Chapter One

'Argh!' Romy screamed as she sat on the edge of the bed. Something under the duvet was moving. She sprung up, her heart beating through her chest, as she floundered around for something to protect herself with.

'What the hell?' came a male voice as someone fumbled on the side table and then switched the lamp on, filling the room with stark brightness.

Romy leaned on the chest of drawers to stop herself keeling over, and blinked rapidly in case she was hallucinating.

A very sleepy and naked-looking man pushed himself out from under the duvet and stood up, making Romy's eyes go wide. It was Luca Bowen.

Thankfully, he was wearing black Calvin Klein boxers, because Romy already felt like she might have a coronary. She was clasping a small vase that she'd grabbed to protect herself with, but now she glanced down at it in disgust. It wouldn't make a dent in his impressive six-pack – but she was still tempted to throw it at his head.

1

'Romy?' he asked in a puzzled voice as he rubbed his eyes. Then he ran a hand through his short black hair, making it all mussed up and sexy. He squinted as if he couldn't quite believe what he was seeing. She faltered for a second and tried to work out why he'd been sleeping soundly – and very rudely – in her bed!

'What are you doing here?' he asked in a gravelly voice.

Her eyebrows rose in shock. 'What am *I* doing here?' she raged, her fists bunching once she'd placed the vase safely back on the set of drawers. Then she took a moment to rein in her anger. She didn't know if it was the adrenaline from the fright that was making her feel like she'd just run a marathon, or the sight of the very uninvited Luca in her bedroom. 'What the hell are you doing in my bed?'

She stomped over to stand straight in front of him, and then wished she hadn't because he was over six feet tall to her five eight, and her chin was now remarkably close to his naked chest.

'Your bed?' he asked in confusion, before his big brown eyes focused back on her and humour sparked in his eyes. 'Is this a joke to get me back for my comments about your ridiculous duck tea boat?' His eyes scanned down and noted her black silky pyjama shorts set and he frowned.

'Stop messing around,' snapped Romy. 'Get out of here!'

'I'm not going anywhere,' he retorted. 'This is my bed.'

'It isn't!' she bit back. 'I moved in yesterday. It's definitely mine.'

Luca frowned again and then turned to look in confusion at the simple sage green duvet set he'd just climbed out of.

'You can't have,' insisted Luca, making no move to put on any clothes, so she picked up a black T-shirt that had been discarded on the back of a chair and threw it at his head as she backed away.

It had been a long day and the last thing she needed was Luca messing about with her already exhausted mind. He did that most days anyway. She knew he hated her little business, a houseboat moored at the end of the garden belonging to her new landlady, Clara.

After moving back to the pretty little village she'd grown up in over a year ago now, Romy had bought a five-year lease on the tea boat by the river in Windsor on a whim. However she found living there uncomfortable because the bedrooms were all used for storage. Clara had persuaded her to move in with her as her lodger, after a few break-ins along the river. When Romy had first moored the boat, its position opposite the dock where Luca and his brother Alex Bowen ran their cruise liners hadn't seemed an issue. She'd felt lucky to have such an accommodating landlady. Unfortunately, Luca had taken umbrage at her 'eyesore' of a boat, and he enjoyed telling her about his issues most days. The man was insufferable!

A handful of ducks had taken up residence on the bow. Romy found them charming, but Luca thought they were a health hazard. Leaving as much mess as she could to wind him up was getting tiring, but she wouldn't let anyone tell her what to do again. She'd left docile Romy back in Essex with her broken heart and duplicitous ex. She'd adored living there, but now she felt she could never return.

'This is my grandmother's house,' said Luca, clearly exasperated at her, as usual. Romy felt as though all the air had been knocked out of her lungs, and glanced around in confusion. Was she in the wrong house?

'Wait a minute. Clara is your grandmother?' she snorted incredulously, then saw that he was serious. She thought back to the number of times she'd sat in deckchairs on the dock with Clara in the early morning, before she opened the tea boat up to dog walkers. Clara loved an early morning coffee and a teacake, or thick slices of buttery toast with marmalade, which was about the extent of Romy's culinary talents and her tea boat menu. Romy had often spent this time venting to her new friend about the 'bloody Bowen brothers and their stupid posh boats!' She cringed inside and bit her lip, wanting to run and hide under the duvet – but this was still her room, and Luca had just got out of her bed!

Romy seethed because Luca and his older brother, Alex, ran modern cruise liners operating tours along this stretch of the river. They went from the castle nestling amongst the trees, up to a popular racecourse and back again. They also ran cruises sailing away from town, towards Romy's grandparents' house, which was also beside the river. Romy's grandad's best friend, Joe, ran *Bertha*, the only steamship on the river.

The rivalry between Joe and the Bowens had simmered for years. Alex and Luca wanted to scoop up *Bertha*, modernise her and run her themselves. But why would you modernise a steamboat? Half of the charm was the old-world glamour that *Bertha* had in buckets, from her crystal chandeliers to the Art Deco bar selling a *Bertha* classic, strawberry gin and lemonade. She was a floating master-piece that drew tourists from miles around. She often featured in travel magazines and social media images, too. *Bertha* had even had a plethora of famous visitors, like Dame Rosalie Alton, their local megastar.

Romy had been inside Clara's bungalow a few times before she moved in, but had never seen a photo of Luca. Maybe Clara despised him as much as Romy did? Romy would have run a mile if she'd realised they were related. She frowned. Clara had never once mentioned she knew either of the brothers. This was so bizarre – although Romy would never acknowledge Luca if he was in her family, either. He was a constant pain in the backside. Maybe Clara felt the same. It didn't explain why he was in her bed, though. Romy felt the burn of humiliation, which made her anger flare as she glared at him mutinously. He still hadn't put his T-shirt on and she looked at it pointedly.

'Look. This is my bed now. I'm exhausted after a long day and I need sleep.'

'So do I,' he stated, rolling his eyes at her – like he did most days.

'Have you been busy fending off hordes of admirers all day on the boat, as usual?' she scoffed sarcastically. Alex and Luca's Italian good looks made women simper and drool around them, and it annoyed the hell out of Romy for some reason.

'I've been at the hospital all evening with *Nonna*,' Luca stated drily, his voice suddenly filling with emotion.

Romy gawped, her hand going to her mouth. 'You mean Clara? What happened? Is she ok?' She dropped all her angst and began rummaging around for the clothes that she'd been wearing earlier. She'd only moved in the day before, so most of her things were still on the boat. In her hurry she completely forgot Luca was there, and pulled her silky pyjama top off and threw her T-shirt back on. Then she froze. She turned back to him. His eyes were out on stalks. 'Stop staring!'

'Stop getting naked,' He retorted, mirroring her movements by pulling his own T-shirt over his head. 'Where are we going?'

'To see Clara, of course,' she said, as if he were a complete idiot.

'Romy... it's 2am.' Luca's shoulders sagged and she looked at the clock on the wall.

'Is the hospital closed for the night?'

'It is,' humour sparked in his eyes again. 'Visiting time finished hours ago.'

'I need to see her. What happened?' she asked.

'I didn't realise you were so close,' he said. She swung around to see if he was being sarcastic, but he just looked exhausted. 'She had a fall. They think she might have broken her hip. She needs an X-ray. My brother is with her. They sent me home in the end because I was pacing the corridors and annoying everyone.'

'I can't imagine that,' she snapped waspishly.

He groaned and sat on the edge of the bed, which made her feel like angry little ants were marching up her spine. However tired she'd been a minute ago, she was now wide awake.

'Can I see her in the morning? She visits me most days on the boat. She insisted I move in here after the recent break-in,' Romy said.

'There was another break-in?' Luca jumped up again and began pacing the room.

It had little in it, except a queen size bed, a chair, mirror and chest of drawers. That suited Romy, as she hated clutter. Her previous job as a vet had meant everything had to be scrupulously clean, but her standards had slipped a little since she'd been home. She thought back to the beautiful veterinary practice she'd run with her long-term partner, Aaron, before that had all gone horribly wrong, and she flinched.

'Why didn't she tell me about it?' Luca asked.

'She probably didn't want to worry you,' Romy soothed, catching his arm and feeling solid muscle, then hastily letting go. She shook herself. Why was she being kind to a guy who complained about her business almost daily? She already knew it was a mess – that she was a mess. She didn't need him to constantly remind her that her decisions were bad and her boat was a blot on the landscape. It was her past choices that had got her into this predicament.

'I need sleep,' he growled, rubbing his eyes. She couldn't deny that he was a hard worker, always the first at the dock and the last to leave. Not that she'd noticed...

'So do I,' parried Romy. 'You'll have to go somewhere else.'

'I can't. I promised *Nonna* I'd stay in the bungalow tonight. Now I bet it was because of the break-in.'

'But she knew I'd be here,' said Romy in exasperation.

'I guess she forgot,' he shrugged. 'What with breaking her hip and everything,' he added, deadpan. Then the light of mischief came into his eyes. 'Although she probably knows you need looking after.'

Her eyes sparked with fire and she stomped her feet. 'Get out of my bed!'

'It's my bed, and I've stayed in it since I was about three years old! I have first dibs.'

'Sleep in Clara's bed.'

'No way! That's weird. Plus, she's the size of a sparrow and has a tiny single bed now. I always joke that she must have bought it from the children's section, but she said the marital bed felt lonely without *Nonno* – my grandad.' He rubbed his eyes in exhaustion for a moment and Romy's bottom lip wobbled. Clara often spoke about how much she missed her husband, who had passed away years previously.

'You sleep in it,' he added, and just like that the fire was back.

'No way! That's weird,' she parroted. 'She's my land-lady. It wouldn't be right to take her bed... and besides, I'm almost as tall as you.' He looked at her sceptically and she huffed. 'We can't both sleep here.'

'We'll have to. Look. We're both clearly exhausted and I'm guessing you're too tired to try and jump my bones, so I can sleep safely,' he joked.

She scoffed in disgust. 'I wouldn't "jump your bones" if you were the last man on earth!' she retorted and he grabbed his heart and pretended to be wounded by her comments as he snuggled up under the duvet again and pulled the covers up to his chin. 'What are you doing?' she asked in horror as he stripped off under the duvet and threw his T-shirt on the floor.

'I need sleep, Romy! I've been in Accident and Emergency at the hospital for over twelve hours, and I intend to get at least a bit of sleep before I head back there. Our team will have to manage the boats without me tomorrow. Alex will want to see her again too. Our parents live in Italy, so she only has us.'

Romy knew how close Luca and Alex were, so she bet she wouldn't be getting much sleep either, if they were early risers. Tomorrow was Monday, the only day her tea boat was shut. She could already feel her eyelids drooping. She glanced at the cosy bed that she'd been dreaming of snuggling into for hours, after attending to a poorly duck that she'd just saved from a fox. Her profession in her past life seemed to be creeping into her new one lately, though she'd tried to leave it behind when things imploded thanks to her ex-boyfriend, Aaron, and his web of lies. She was determined never to rely on anyone again. That way, if life fell apart, she'd have no one to blame but herself.

With a big theatrical sigh, she grumpily sat on the opposite side of the bed to Luca and glared at him, but he was already snoring soundly. She gave him a shove and he gratifyingly moved over and shut up, his dark lashes brushing his cheek in sleep. How could someone so annoying go from argumentative to angelic in seconds, she wondered. He must be worn out, or he'd still be sparring with her like usually did.

She was too tired and worried about Clara to think deeply about why her landlady hadn't told her who her grandsons were. But then, if Romy were related to Luca, she would certainly have disowned him too.

Chapter Two

Romy woke up from the soundest sleep she'd had in ages, then froze as an arm was thrown over her chest and she was snuggled into someone's groin. She blinked a few times to clear her foggy mind.

She'd opened up her tea boat with no experience, but a lot of determination. It had been a steep learning curve. She aimed to establish a routine while helping her new neighbour, Greg, whose boat had been broken into a couple of nights earlier. There had been a spate of these break-ins over the past year. That, and the lack of a proper bedroom on the boat, had resulted in Romy giving in to pressure from the family and accepting Clara's kind offer of room and board. Becoming friends with Clara had been one of the joys of moving back home. Her friend was a sea of calm after the turbulence of Romy's bonkers family, who lived at various points along the river near the town.

Trying to recall if she'd met someone in a bar and brought them home, Romy knew that definitely wasn't her usual style. Loneliness had surrounded her for a while, though, she admitted to herself. Although incredibly gorgeous, she still hoped it wasn't Greg from next door. Apart from a short-lived but fun encounter with a bartender last year, she'd essentially given up on men. He hadn't wanted anything serious, so he'd been a perfect distraction.

Shuffling towards the edge of the bed, Romy tried to ease the arm away, but only got pulled in closer to a naked chest. Whoever this was, he smelt heavenly – manly and spicy.

Focussing her sleep-deprived mind, she remembered offering to help Greg to clear up the mess from knocked-over bins, and then recalled a poorly duck. With a groan, Romy attempted to untangle limbs, without waking her companion. She'd spent hours patching the duck's wing and settling him into the snug, a little warm space built for the previous owners' dog that had become a duck haven. Hence Luca's disparaging duck boat comments.

Luca! She sat bolt upright and pulled the duvet off him, which she hastily shoved back because he was still half-naked.

He woke up and rubbed his eyes groggily, a slow grin spreading on his lips when he noticed her next to him, which rapidly changed when he saw her sitting with her arms crossed over her chest and her eyes spitting fire.

'Good morning,' he drawled, sleepily.

'Keep your hands to yourself!' she raged.

He seemed to realise for the first time he was hogging quite a lot of the bed. 'What can I say,' he shrugged. 'I'm a snuggler. I guess I'm not so choosy when I'm exhausted,' he said.

The words stung, but she attacked back. 'You aren't choosy at all,' she shook her head. 'You have a different woman hanging on your every word most days.'

His eyes zeroed in on her. 'You've been watching me?'

he tutted. 'Naughty Romy,' he said in his lilting Italian accent that made her toes curl. It was an involuntary response to such a dreamy language and not her fault, she reasoned. She closed her eyes, trying to re-centre, pretending he wasn't there. No one else seemed to make her want to erupt with anger like he did. He infuriated her! She felt incensed at the stupidity of all the women who threw themselves at Alex and Luca on a regular basis.

'I can't help but see. Your fancy cruise liners keep parking opposite my tea boat.'

'That is where we've always moored,' he drawled sardonically, sitting up and letting the covers fall to his hips, making her mouth go dry... another involuntary response. She huffed and stood up and then wished she hadn't because he looked appreciatively at her legs.

'My boat is closed today. When can I see Clara?' she asked.

'The duck tea boat you mean?' he raised an eyebrow and she ignored him, searching around for her clothes, whilst picking up a few of his and throwing them his way, hoping he'd take the hint and leave.

Her boat seemed to attract birds. Swans floated by, hoping to be thrown titbits. Ducks had also nested on the stern of the boat. When ducks begun laying eggs there, there wasn't anything Romy could do. Law fully protected nests and the eggs and she actually loved seeing the mother ducks incubating their brood. The mallards sat on their eggs for almost a month and only left them fleetingly to feed. Romy was finding more and more people coming to her boat to see them. The same thing had happened last year, and it seemed ducks talked to each other – this year there were even more of them! She'd had to block the area off with a few pieces of wood, but she knew this wasn't ideal.

Customers seemed to adore watching the ducks while they drank tea, or the strong coffee she bought from a small local artisan company. All she'd wanted was space to escape from her past and provide a roof over her head, but now she was looking after the welfare of about twenty ducks, some swans and a few Egyptian geese! She sighed and puffed out her cheeks in frustration.

'Stop calling it the duck tea boat! I've told you I'm not getting rid of the ducks. They were here first.'

Luca rolled his eyes in exasperation. This was an old argument. He thought her boat was an embarrassment and a blot on the admittedly picturesque local landscape. The cobbled street that ran into town, with its stone and glass fronted cafés and beautiful shops, some of which were built, or later extended, in the Stuart period and Victorian era, had become a Mecca for tourists. The street ran up to the majestic castle nestled amongst the trees, which could also be seen from the river.

She couldn't care less what Luca thought. The more he complained, the more she dug her heels in and left the messy exterior. It certainly didn't seem to put off the dog walkers who flocked to her boat each day.

'I can't believe Clara is related to you,' she said scathingly. Then she gulped, because daylight was filtering through the curtains and Luca moved to stand in front of her in just his boxers. Wow, he was gorgeous, she thought tetchily. Shame he was such a prima donna. She hastily looked away and began picking up his clothes from the chair and floor to shove into his arms. 'You're not exactly tidy yourself,' she pointed out, inclining her head to his pile of clothes.

'I was in a hurry to get to bed.'

'So was I, but there was an annoying interloper in it.'

Luca sighed wearily and brushed his mussed-up hair out of his eyes. Seeing him ruffled was unusual, so she enjoyed her tiny victory, then felt a twinge of remorse, as he was clearly stressed and worried about his grandmother.

'Clara?' she asked again.

He glanced at the thick fancy watch on his wrist and began walking towards the bathroom, just when Romy realised she really needed to pee. 'We can go as soon as we're dressed,' he called over his shoulder. 'Visiting starts in thirty minutes.'

'*We?*' she squeaked.

'Both of us are going to the same place. Unless you want me to report back?' He clearly knew Romy well enough to understand her stubborn streak once she'd set her mind on something.

'I guess so. Get dressed quickly then,' she demanded, wishing she could jump in before him and that he'd go away before she had to speak to him again. Now they'd be in the car together and she wouldn't be able to have a frank and honest conversation with Clara about the fibs her landlady had been telling with big, grumpy, Luca hovering at her shoulder.

'I need to see for myself that your relationship with *Nonna* is what you say it is,' he added bluntly. 'Why are you really living in her home?'

'You don't believe me?' she said incredulously. 'You think I'm motivated by her money?' he shrugged. 'You do know that most of my family are famous and loaded?' she said sarcastically.

Both of her siblings, Maya and Arthur, were recent self-made millionaires, and her grandparents were the darlings of the showbiz world. Her grandmother, Ettie, made clothes for royalty and her grandad, Owen, was a world-renowned exotic plant expert who now had his own television show – and groupies, which her grandmother found hilarious!

'But are you?' he raised an eyebrow and she felt her fingers bunch into a fist. How she'd love to wipe the smile from that smug, handsome face. She'd been the most senior vet at her old practice, after Aaron, but he'd been syphoning off the profits, she'd eventually discovered. She had never been a party animal, spending more time with sick ones instead, but that was none of Luca's business. That he thought she was a gold-digger was hilarious. Money held little interest for her, other than to feed her animals and keep a roof over her head. To be honest, she was probably more comfortable in a barn, snuggled up with the chickens, than in a sterile house with concrete walls. She craved simplicity and didn't judge others on what they had in the bank, unlike some people… She hadn't thought it possible for Luca to annoy her further, but he always surprised her. A light of mischief bubbled up her spine and she decided to make him pay for his thoughtless comments.

'Well,' she fluttered her eyelashes at him, while he frowned. 'I was thinking of finding a sugar daddy, but I bore easily, so perhaps a sugar *Nonna* is the next best thing.'

Luca blanched and his posture went rigid as he regarded her. She gulped because his focus unnerved her still, even when she was winding him up. Electricity crackled in the air whenever they were near each other and it was unsettling. She felt like she needed to stand under an ice-cold shower to regain her senses.

'Then we need to spend more time together,' he decided, clearly pleased with himself. 'So that I can watch over you and make sure you don't get your claws into my grandmother.'

'Um…' she foundered, as he took a step towards her. 'I

don't think that's a good idea. I was joking,' she gulped as he took another step, his eyes never leaving her face.

'Get dressed,' he said shortly and then turned and left the room. Romy heaved a huge sigh of relief, as being in the same space as Luca was not a lot of fun. He filled the room with masculine energy. It was overwhelming at times, which made her prickly.

'Stupid, pig-headed, Italian!' she grumbled, while trying to calm her racing heart... and wondering what would have happened if he'd swept her into his arms instead of always arguing with her.

She sat down heavily on the edge of the bed they'd both just vacated and stared at the closed door. How on earth had her life come to this? He was one of her least favourite people on the planet, yet here he was in her private space. At least she'd survived a night in the same bed as Luca Bowen and come out unscathed... Hadn't she?

Chapter Three

F inding a parking space at the hospital involved Luca doing lots of swearing in Italian under his breath. Romy was finally enjoying herself, as his parking was abysmal. How on earth he docked those huge cruisers was beyond her, and he'd scowled when she'd asked him. She offered to park for him, but he'd ignored her and spent a few minutes messing around with the parking app to pay for the space (or two spaces, if you counted the one next to theirs that he'd slightly parked across), before walking off in a huff at such a pace that she'd had to run to keep up with him.

They exited the lift, and she watched the nurses perk up at the sight of him and sit straighter. She rolled her eyes in disgust. What was it about a six foot four Adonis that made women lose their minds? Maybe it was the Italian good looks or the dark brooding smile, but as soon as he noted the nurses, he was charm personified. Someone allowed them to see Clara, even though they were a few minutes early for visiting time. Romy might as well have been invisible, and she bristled.

Following him into a side room, she found Clara propped up in bed with blue and white bed sheets pulled up to her waist. Her usually sunny and bright smile was missing, and her eyes were closed. Her pale skin made Romy feel extra-worried because she was usually so vibrant and full of life. Romy exchanged worried glances with Luca and they both moved forward quickly, to stand on either side of the bed and take a hand each.

Clara's eyes fluttered open and she smiled and winced as she tried to sit up. Luca immediately helped ease her into a sitting position.

'Luca. Thank you,' she said as she tried to settle herself comfortably. 'Romy, I didn't expect to see you here. What about the duck tea boat?'

'It's not a duck tea boat!' she glanced at Luca as if to say the name was his fault, and he shrugged and grinned, pulling up a chair to sit next to his gran. Romy did the same and looked around at the room. Other than the hospital bed, a couple of chairs, and a drip that was attached to Clara's arm, the room was pretty sparse.

'I'm not working today,' Romy said, determined not to tell Clara about the new break-in next door. She smiled reassuringly at her. 'I just wanted to see if you were ok.'

'There was another break-in,' stated Luca, making Romy wish it was him connected up to a drip, so that she could turn it off! Now Clara would be full of anxiety! She glared at him mutinously and he ignored her.

'Oh no! Where?' asked Clara in alarm.

'The boat next to Romy's,' he said.

She didn't know how he'd got that information, because she'd only found out herself when she'd gone back to her boat to collect a few things. It was petty vandalism, but she was worried about the birds and their nests, especially now that Clara had persuaded her to move into the bungalow with her. Maybe she should move back, or fit a gate.

'It's fine,' soothed Romy, patting Clara's hand gently. 'It was just a bin that got knocked over, and some beer cans thrown onto the deck. There was a broken window, but no one actually got into the boat after all. I helped clear it up, so I was late getting back last night. The new guy next door is lovely,' she said pointedly, looking at Luca who smiled tightly. 'Quite sexy too,' she added for good measure, winking at Clara. She laughed and then winced again, as her hip must be hurting. Romy decided she'd have to rein in the jokes for the moment.

'Thank goodness you moved in!' said Clara. 'Otherwise you might have been there and got hurt.'

'I can look after myself.'

'I know that,' said Clara, shaking her head at Luca, who looked as bemused as Romy felt. 'But I think of you as my granddaughter. I have six strapping grandsons and I need some balance,' she laughed at her own joke and then flinched again, so Romy got up to settle her more comfortably.

'You need to look after yourself more,' Romy said, while Clara gave Luca a pert look. He seemed as confused as Romy was.

'I'm so relieved that you're both staying at the bungalow now,' Clara sighed, closing her eyes for a minute. Luca and Romy exchanged glances. It seemed neither knew what she was on about. When she opened her eyes, Romy noticed a glint of determination in them that hadn't been there before.

'Umm... Just to clarify. Luca won't be staying there...' Romy said.

Clara smiled weakly. 'My hip operation is later today

and it will be four or five days before I can come home. Luca promised me he'd stay until I got back, didn't you Luca?'

She looked at him expectantly, and he spluttered.

'But that was before I knew you'd taken on a lodger, *Nonna...*' he said patiently. 'Romy can look after the bungalow for a few days.'

'But the break-ins! I'm so worried,' said Clara, her voice wobbling.

Romy frowned. Clara had said after the first break-ins that she'd hit the thieves over the head with a baseball bat if they ever dared to enter her property. She wasn't afraid of anything! Maybe the fall had made her feel more vulnerable, though? Romy was worried, and quickly picked up Clara's hand.

'*Nonna,*' Luca reasoned, taking her other hand again. 'I live in Mayfair.'

'I know,' she shivered. 'Such a cold place.'

Luca spluttered and Romy tried not to laugh. It seemed she was witnessing a master of manipulation at work. Her own family was prone to a bit of insider pressure, so it was fascinating to watch it in another family – especially if it made Luca uncomfortable. It was intriguing to find out more about the fancy central London flat he lived in. He went back there every night according to Maya, Romy's sister, who was acquainted with the brothers. But he was always first to arrive on the dock in the morning. Romy knew that herself, as her boat was moored opposite and she was an early riser. Because of the vandals, she was extra vigilant, she reasoned.

'It's a penthouse flat,' he argued. 'I just don't like trinkets and clutter like you do, as you well know.'

'Luca!' gasped Romy at his rudeness. Romy would

never speak to her own precious Ettie like that. As a child, she'd have been sent to her room. And she wouldn't dare as an adult, either. Her grandmother was as soft as butter, but had an underlying layer of steel.

'Sorry,' Luca hung his head and leaned in to kiss his gran's cheek, but she brushed him away. 'What do you need me to do?' he asked.

A light of mischief instantly appeared in Clara's eyes and Romy watched as the 'frail pensioner' got her own way.

'I want you to stay at my home with Romy until I'm well enough to return.'

'Really? For all that time?' he questioned, his eyes still dipped, as if he was about to step into the dentist's chair and have a tooth extracted.

Clara shrugged noncommittally and then clapped her hands happily. 'Good. I'm told I should keep my stress levels low before my operation and I don't want to be worrying about another break-in.'

'We could just set up security cameras, or an alarm?' suggested Romy hopefully. She couldn't think of anything worse than another night with Luca. Where the hell would he sleep? Neither of them could reasonably fit into Clara's tiny bed – she'd checked. 'My brother, Arthur, is setting up CCTV on my boat today, so he could pop by the bungalow too. You know he's a tech guy?' she asked Luca and he nodded. They'd met quite a few times as the whole family visited *Bertha* and Joe regularly for steamboat trips up and down the river. Romy liked strutting past the Bowen brothers' boats and straight onto *Bertha* to wind Luca up. It was a fascinating hobby.

'Ow,' winced Clara as she tried to reach the water glass a nurse had left on the trolley at the end of her bed.

Luca sprang up immediately and asked her if she needed anything else, refilling her cup and passing to her.

'I'll think about it,' she assured him and Romy, once she had sipped the water and settled back down. 'But for now, I just need my beauty sleep.'

'Of course!' said Romy, backing out of the room. Luca gently kissed his grandmother's cheek, but she'd already closed her eyes and dismissed them.

Romy was so confused! Clara was usually sweetness and light. Luca gave his gran one more look over his shoulder, in case she woke up and told them both it was all a joke, Romy guessed. He sighed and followed Romy into the brightly lit corridor with the gaggle of giggly nurses who were looking Luca's way and tittering. Romy glowered at them and then felt mean. They might need a little fun in their day, when they worked so hard. Even if it was in the shape of a Bowen brother, who would break their hearts and then not give them a second thought, no doubt.

'Clara can't be serious, can she?' she asked under her breath, leaning back against the cool white wall.

'She is.' Luca's shoulders sagged in defeat.

'We could... just tell her you stayed?' Romy suggested.

'What? As in lie?'

'Ummm. More of a little fib,' she hedged, wondering why he was so angry.

'No,' he stated firmly, deep frown lines on his forehead. 'I made a promise to my grandmother. Feel free to move out if you want, but I'm staying.'

'There's only one bed big enough for anyone over five foot two. Believe me, I measured Clara's bed this morning.' Luca rolled his eyes at her dramatics. 'There's nowhere to sleep on my boat, all the extra space is used for storage. It was never meant as living quarters. The whole middle floor is a tearoom, as you well know. I'm not moving out. I just moved in!'

'Then it looks like we've both just landed a flatmate for a few days,' Luca said.

'You'll have to sleep on the couch,' Romy reasoned.

'Have you seen *Nonna*'s couch? It barely fits her backside on it!'

'The floor, then.'

'It's stone! Was it so terrible to share?' he asked, his lip quirking upwards suddenly.

'What do you think?' she answered pertly. 'I'm a paying guest.'

'Has she taken any money from your account yet?' he asked.

Romy frowned and got her phone out of her jeans pocket, then checked her banking app. She wrinkled her nose. Most people would be glad that their rent hadn't gone out yet, but this just complicated things. 'Not yet,' she admitted.

'Well. It seems that until it does, we are both guests. We will share the double bed,' he said a touch too loudly and a couple of young nurses giggled. He held a hand up to silence Romy's protestations. 'I won't touch you and you won't touch me.'

'I woke up with your arm around me this morning,' she stated dryly. He frowned as if he was trying to recall – which infuriated her further.

'It won't happen again... until you ask me to,' he added with a wink.

She rolled her eyes and stomped off up the corridor and into the lift, where she shut the door before he could step inside. She had to wait for him at the car, though, because she didn't have keys. He arrived with a steaming cup of coffee, which made her mouth water.

'That was childish,' he said. Then he got into the car, not opening the central locking until he was comfortably behind the wheel.

'*That* was childish,' she parroted when she could finally get in, but couldn't help but grin and their eyes met in mirth.

He lifted his coffee and revealed an empty cup underneath, then proceeded to pour half his drink into it. Then he handed it to her.

'Your face was a picture when you saw the coffee,' he joked. She gratefully took the second cup and sipped it. 'I noticed yesterday that they are pretty generous with their coffee offering.' She looked at him from under her lashes and grinned finally.

'You need to visit the duck tea boat for a hot drink, instead of a reprimand,' she teased. 'We sell the best coffee in town.'

He quirked an eyebrow. 'I might just do that one day. Home?'

'Home,' she agreed, as he started the car up and headed back towards the river.

Chapter Four

Luca tried not to stare at Romy's legs as she walked around in her little pyjama shorts set. They'd ordered a takeaway and managed to eat it together in his grandmother's cosy kitchen without killing each other. They were both putting off going to bed, he could tell, but there was only one couch. If Romy sat down, they'd practically be on top of each other. There was a beanbag *Nonna* had bought online, but it was under-stuffed, or he was too heavy for it. He'd learned to his detriment that there weren't enough foam beans inside because he'd once slid off the side of the thing. His grandmother was obsessed with shopping sites! He'd opened a kitchen drawer to find it filled with 'useful' kitchen items she'd bought online and never used. So far, he'd discovered five whisks, a tiny nutmeg grater, two spoon rests and a bagel cutter.

He usually sat instead at the small breakfast bar in the open plan room that was a kitchen, diner and living space. His grandfather had knocked out most of the internal walls so that they could see the boats from anywhere inside the bungalow, but it did mean they were never away from work.

When *Nonno* had passed, Luca and Alex had decided to come and help Clara. The only other option would have been to sell the business their grandparents had built up for years. No one wanted this to happen, and it all had coincided with Luca needing to relocate to the U.K. for personal reasons. It wasn't something he ever talked about. His heart hadn't healed. He didn't think it ever would. Who needed love when you were busy, though, right?

'Do you want to watch a movie?' he asked and Romy froze on the spot. If either of them went to bed first, then the other would disturb them later, so they would have to go together, like a real couple, which they weren't.

'Is that what you usually do with your dates at your fancy Mayfair apartment?' she asked, but she did walk towards him and snuggle into the couch, which meant the beanbag was left for him. He scowled at it and wished he'd kept his mouth shut.

'Wouldn't you like to know?' he replied, as he tried to get comfortable and she smirked at his long legs sticking off the end.

'Not really,' she gave him a saccharine-sweet smile and then jumped up and headed towards the kitchen. He watched her go and couldn't help but lick his lips. There was something about this woman that riled the hell out of him. He wanted to grab her and make her see sense, or kiss her senseless, which he worried was more his thought process lately. He'd never hurt a woman in his life – even Bianca, who had pushed him to the limits of sanity. Romy's plump kissable lips were on his mind a lot and it was making him grumpier than ever. Having to share a bed with her was torture!

'I bought popcorn,' she told him happily, as she showed him the huge bowl she was carrying. She was so gorgeous when she smiled, but equally appealing when her eyes were shooting daggers at him.

'Can we share the couch?' he asked and she looked at it as if working out the logistics. They'd have to be pretty close to squeeze in.

'How does Clara manage when she has guests?' asked Romy. 'I've only been in a few times because she visits me on the boat for tea and toast, or a teacake, most mornings.'

'We usually congregate around the breakfast bar. Most of our family are still in Italy, so it's only Alex and me who visit, or *Nonna*'s friends. Now you too, I guess.'

'How come you ended up here?' she asked. His face became guarded, which she must have picked up. She put the popcorn on the little table next to the couch and held her hands up in surrender. 'Sorry I asked!'

'It's ok,' he said, getting up and sitting on the couch so she had to wriggle in next to him for them both to have room. Normally on a date, he'd be pulling her into the crook of his arm and possibly pressing his lips to the curve of her neck by now. He wished Romy would stop wriggling! 'When *Nonno* passed we didn't want *Nonna* to be lonely. She's stubborn, as you know,' he grinned suddenly and Romy matched his smile. 'She didn't want to leave her home. She was born here and it's why they settled back in Windsor, I guess. They used to travel back home to us in Italy all the time.'

'I can see the appeal of the river, but swapping Italy for this?' she looked around in confusion. The little cottage was solid and dependable, with roses winding around the door and the beds and borders of the garden bursting with flowers. 'I mean more the weather, than the actual place. This is beautiful,' she clarified.

'It's tiny,' he laughed.

'How much space does one person need?' she replied.

He shrugged, quite liking the feel of her thigh next to his. 'Clearly not much,' he grinned. He tried to relax his shoulders and not shift his backside in case she moved. This was torture! She arched one eyebrow his way, but he refused to respond. He clicked the television on and started scrolling through their movie choices.

'Do you have a preference?'

'Just nothing mushy,' she ground out and his lips quirked.

'An action movie it is then,' he chuckled, pinching a handful of popcorn and stuffing it in his mouth to stop himself from kissing her.

Chapter Five

Romy was having the most amazing dream. She stretched out and opened her eyes and then blinked in shock. Her face was pressed up against a hard, muscled chest. She looked up into Luca's sardonic brown eyes and pushed her hands against naked skin with a yelp. 'We definitely need a discussion on boundaries,' he chuckled, amusement in his tone. It had been a long time since she'd shared a bed with a man and muscle memory meant she had clearly snuggled into his chest at night without meaning to.

'I'm so sorry!' she flushed, swinging her legs out of the bed in mortification, after she'd scolded him for exactly the same thing the previous morning.

'I kind of liked it,' he chuckled and her skin tinged red as she silently fumed. Luca would milk this all day. They'd finally agreed to get on with it and share the bed, but equally had pinky-sworn not to breathe a word about it to anyone else. Maya would find the whole blackmailing *Nonna* story hilarious, given the extremes their own grandmother, Ettie, went to, to get her own way. Her older brother, Arthur, was another matter. He'd be yanking Romy out of the bungalow, even though Luca was the same age as him, at thirty, and was certainly a match physically. Luca was toned and had muscles in all the right places from working on the boats, while her brother went to the gym and enjoyed running along the river.

'Let's just forget what happened and get to work,' Romy suggested.

Luca glanced at his watch and swore under his breath. He jumped up and grabbed a towel for a shower. 'I slept in!' he said in alarm.

'Have you ever heard of pyjamas?' she asked reasonably, trying not to stare at his usual Calvins and bare chest. He ginned at her and her stomach went a bit wobbly for a second.

When she noted the shower being turned on, she tried not to picture water cascading off his toned abs. She gulped and began picking up clothes. She scooped up her usual attire of jeans and a fitted T-shirt. She didn't like to primp and preen anymore, and dressed to please no one but herself. It used to take her ages to get ready to go anywhere, but now she wore what was practical and comfortable. She tapped her fingers impatiently on her knee while she waited for Luca and then stepped past him, trying not to reach out to brush a droplet of water from his chest. She really must be sex-starved, judging by the way she was behaving. She hadn't had a proper relationship since Aaron, other than one quick fling, and her body was clearly missing the contact with another human being. Luca was now looking around, trying to find his clothes.

'If you folded them up at night, then you'd know where they were!' she said, watching him in exasperation. He ignored her and pulled up the duvet cover to look under it.

Romy tutted and went to have her shower. Luckily, he hadn't massacred the bathroom. Noting his toothbrush, standing next to hers on the basin, made her take a moment to stop and breathe. It was so intimate, sharing such a personal space. This was a weird parallel universe, compared to her usual life, but he'd be gone in a few days. She had to put up with him until then.

Being meticulously tidy used to be a habit. As a vet, her work and home space had been scrupulously clean, but after her world had fallen apart, she not cared enough to bother what her living space looked like. The new tearoom was pristine for hygiene reasons, but she knew the outside of the boat was a mess. The fact that Luca asked her to clean it up so often made her dig her heels in, but she was tired suddenly.

Her old life has been full – long hours at the practice that she had run with Aaron, and nights with him full of love and passion. She'd believed they were the perfect couple. How naive she'd been. Aaron's days had been filled with lies. After four years together, she'd had no choice but to leave her business and 'friends' behind. Which of them had known, she often wondered? How many of them had been as duplicitous as he had? She was better off on her own. Coming back to the pretty little town in Windsor that she'd grown up in had been painful. Many happy memories had been made here, but she almost felt she was tainting them by returning under such a cloud of shame.

Romy heard Luca moving around and turned to face him. The towel was dipping dangerously low on his hips and could hit the floor at any moment. He caught her staring and a wolfish smile crept onto his lips. 'Want me to scrub your back?' he asked.

'No thanks, I can manage,' she replied tartly, as if this

would be her worst nightmare – which it would. She'd had enough players to last a lifetime and was resolutely off pig-headed men.

Luca had already left by the time she came out, and she felt weirdly bereft. She guessed it was because she was used to her daily chats with Clara and she missed her friend. Dropping a quick text to Clara to say good luck with her operation, Romy hoped she would see it before she went down. Luca had already said he'd take her back to visit Clara when he went later, so she could give her a hug then. Romy sniffed a bit with self-pity, and then stopped in shock. When had Clara pretty much become her only friend? Quickly gathering up her things for work, she swiped a few of Luca's clothes off the bed and folded them neatly on the end of the duvet – then messed them up again angrily. She was not his skivvy.

Strolling down Clara's long garden towards the dock, Romy ran her fingers along the rosemary plants that flanked the path and inhaled the herbal camphor-like scent. She opened the gate and glanced towards town and at the Bowen boats. The sun was up and she let the rays warm her skin for a moment as she listened to the birds sing. A few goldfinches, with their black, yellow and red plumage flew across the water and she followed their trail in the clear blue sky and tried not to wonder if she was looking for a familiar dark head of hair and grumpy face. Traders were setting up their stalls for the day on the cobbled street running up to town. The outdoor weekly market was a new addition, but it was popular. The castle and river cruises brought in a lot of tourists, but the market was a magnet for locals as well. Each stall was brightly festooned with coloured bunting and had a striped awning to shield the products from the British weather. It was looking to be a scorching summer ahead, so Romy felt sure the traders would be glad of the shade from the awnings too.

As she opened up the boat, she accidentally knocked one of the tables with the door and sent a pile of crockery crashing to the ground. Cursing under her breath, she tried not to trip over a mallard duck that had decided to see if she had any food. She gently shooed him out again. He had taken up residence on her floating tearoom, along with a few of his friends.

In Romy's previous life as a vet and girlfriend extraordinaire, she'd have rehomed the duck without breaking a perfectly painted nail and her boyfriend would have told her how amazing she was. That was before she found out he was still sleeping with his not-so-ex-wife, and also pocketing more than his fair share of the profits of the veterinary surgery they'd run together.

Now she kind of liked the way the unkempt, nosy duck had made himself at home on her boat. He seemed to like bobbing his head out of corners and scaring the life out of her, so the name Bob had stuck. Putting lots of potted plants on the roof of the long boat had felt whimsical at the time, but now the birds had made themselves comfortable between them and she was loath to shove them off. They seemed to have their own fan club of dog walkers.

An idea sparked in her brain and she gave a wicked smile. Luca would hate it, which made her determined to follow through on the scheme. She pictured the boat freshly jet sprayed and painted in duck egg blue tones, with gold metalwork and branding spelling out *The Duck Boat*. Luca liked teasing her about the name because of the birds on board, so that's what she'd call it, and he'd have to stare at it forever!

She often found herself absently feeding the ducks

while she thought about her ex, Aaron. She had racked her brain about how he'd managed to keep his two lives separate. Surely someone at the practice must have known that Aaron was still sleeping with his wife and kept it to themselves? His wife must have called the practice, for instance. She lived in Wales, near his original practice. She was just far enough away not to be able to pop into their new place in Essex. Aaron spent his time between both businesses. There was no way he could have fooled everybody. That was the kind of secret that burned inside, so she couldn't imagine that anyone who did know hadn't told others. Humiliation swirled around in her stomach when she thought of her ex. Feeling tears prick the back of her eyes, she refused to let them fall. She had been such an idiot. Dating someone already taken wasn't her style, she'd never knowingly do that. That was why Aaron had told her he was divorced, she guessed. The fact that he'd expected her to accept the situation, when she finally found out what was going on, meant that he'd never really known her at all.

Romy recalled scampering home with her tail between her legs to her grandparents' huge house and rambling garden, situated further up the river in Windsor. Romy, Maya and their brother, Arthur, had each had an outbuilding in the garden when they were young and Romy loved hers the best. Her barn had always been full of straw, smelly animals and lots of poo. She chuckled at the memory. The place was cleaned out every day, but the menagerie of stray ducks, birds, lizards and her grandparents' old dog had definitely left its own unique scent. The siblings would lie on their tummies and look out across the water through the window, telling each other their hopes and dreams from the small hay loft in the barn. Calling it a barn was a stretch, it was actually a glorified shed, but Romy loved it anyway.

Moving in with their grandparents when Romy was about ten meant the siblings had clung together. Their bond had strengthened while they adapted and learned to cope. Their grandparents, Ettie and Owen, were incredible, but also batty and incorrigible and always up to mischief! Not letting the children dwell on their parents' absence for long, they had had swept them into their world of creativity, tea parties and adventure. Every room in their house seemed to have a thousand books lining the walls.

Romy smiled, remembering the floral scent of her grandmother's perfume when she enveloped her in a hug, when her mother left them. Romy had called out to her and seen her mother turn. There had been anguish in her eyes as she brushed tears from her cheeks, but her dad had carefully guided her back to their car, his own face ashen and set in hard lines. Romy knew how important their work as surgeons for a medical charity abroad was, but she'd never quite understood how they could leave their young children. She had always resolved she would never do that to her own children, but that was irrelevant now. Trying for four long years to conceive with Aaron meant that babies were not going to be part of her future. Acceptance of that fact had been hard. She certainly didn't intend ever to fall in love again. It hurt. Plus she'd been prodded and poked around by doctors for years, without any real resolution, and she was too exhausted to have to explain to a new partner who might want a child of their own.

Aaron already had two children. Clearly he was capable, but it had never happened for her. Filling her days instead with nurturing injured animals and her boyfriend hadn't worked out well, either.

Romy gazed around and noted the peeling paint, crumbling handrails and bowed floorboards of her boat. Sighing, she got out the dustpan and brush and began sweeping up the mess of broken crockery she'd made, which just added to the greater shambles that was her tea boat.

The compact kitchen was spotless, and she'd made cute seating areas on the bow and the deck outside, by the little private berth she'd rented for the next five years from Clara. Six tables were dotted around the inside of the boat.

Dog walkers flocked to the pathway between Clara's bungalow and Romy's tea boat. The tea boat was a pit stop, as this side of the river led up to a few rows of houses and then acres of fields and open land near the popular racecourse. The course was on the other side of the river, but could be accessed via various bridges along the route.

Romy went outside and looked across the water. The smile slid from her face as she pictured Clara walking down the dock a few days ago, in a long flowing pink dress and matching fitted cardigan, a flower clipped in her short grey hair.

'You ok?' she had asked Romy, as she'd settled herself in one of the chairs on the deck. Romy didn't know why Clara picked up the small laminated menu because she always chose the same thing, a latte and a thick buttery teacake with marmalade. Romy had given her a warm hug. She felt a smile unfurling now at the memory.

'It's those dratted boys,' she'd grumbled to Clara. 'Luca's always scowling at me across the water.'

Her landlady's eyes had sparkled. 'They do seem to be a bit of a pain.'

Now Romy rolled her eyes. Clara had loved hearing about how naughty the Bowen brothers were. Why hadn't she admitted they were her grandchildren? Romy wondered again.

Bob the duck had been preening. 'He's a princess,' Clara had joked. Romy couldn't disagree. She had glanced back over the dock. Luca had been standing there, looking her way.

Clara had chuckled and sipped her coffee. 'Why don't you both talk it through and come up with a solution?' she'd asked Romy. 'He can't be all bad.'

Romy had raised an eyebrow at this and Clara had laughed and held her hands up in surrender.

Chapter Six

Romy watched a gaggle of women hovering around Luca and simpering at his every word as he led them towards his boat. She growled under her breath at the lunacy. Alex was ok, she supposed, but Luca was a menace.

Both men had that Italian charm, with dark hair and eyes that seemed to swallow you up whole. Their toned bodies, from hours of punishing work on the boats, were often on show while they cleaned the outside of the cruisers in between tours – that drew as much of a crowd as the tours did!

Romy shook her head in disgust and then opened the pedal bin to slide a broken coffee mug inside, which made Bob jump from his sleeping place by the door. He seemed to enjoy listening to her muttering to herself and was quite tame. Romy couldn't help but laugh as he gave her a pert stare to tell her off before he toddled off, tail feathers twitching. He seemed to like being wherever she was. She hoped he hadn't had too hard a life. He was definitely missing some tail feathers. She actually liked his company, but she'd never tell him that or he'd completely take over her world. At the moment, he slept on the boat for a few hours during the day, but he was gradually spending more time with her.

Her parents and grandparents had never questioned the way she'd come home and dropped her previous life, but she knew it worried them. The village veterinary surgery had asked her to join them, but she didn't want to go back to that routine. It was costing her a fortune to look after the ducks and the wildlife around her boat, though. She had to keep the tea boat up to cover all that. The owner of the village vets was a handsome guy with twinkly eyes called Jeremy, but she was definitely not in the market for good-looking men with bags of charm and a good bedside manner (she guessed) – not that she'd thought about him much. The last thing she needed in her life was another vet boyfriend, however much she enjoyed chatting to him and asking his advice about the birds.

'You should contact the local swan sanctuary,' he'd advised when she'd last called him. He had given her the number, which she'd scribbled down on a scrap of paper.

'Thanks, Jeremy.'

'You sure we can't tempt you to join us here?' he'd cajoled.

She'd laughed. 'Not right now, the ducks need me,' she'd said, rolling her eyes at Bob, who had just strolled past the door. Jeremy had chuckled at her words.

'I must pop by and meet them sometime.'

Romy paused and then grinned to herself. Was Jeremy flirting with her? She had no clue about that these days, and second-guessed everything. 'Please do,' she'd said. 'I might even throw in a free cupcake,' she added, before thanking him for the number and saying goodbye.

The complete change of pace had actually been a

blessed relief, after years at university and then the punishing hours running her old practice. She adored animals, but had been starting to feel burnt out in her old life. Aaron had brushed over it when she'd brought it up and she'd been made to feel like she was being dramatic.

What she hadn't imagined was that the tea boat would be so popular. A steady stream of customers didn't give her time to update the vessel. She only sold thick buttery slabs of toast, teacakes, biscuits, the occasional frosted cupcake (if she could be bothered), tea, coffee and soft drinks. Her secret was a huge coffee machine that she'd bought second hand online, and the big generous teacakes she sold, instead of the tiny ones you often found in cafés. Despite the upkeep of the injured birds that kept turning up, her over-heads weren't crippling, unlike a high street store. The coffee machine was industrial and made coffees immacu-lately and fast. Customers came in droves for that alone.

People loved stepping aboard her converted houseboat. They liked sitting with their pets, enjoying the river views, not the view of her boat (obviously). Luca Bowen seemed to take umbrage about her venue because it was the view his customers got when they stepped aboard. She smirked, but then had a thought. Her boat's current image might also not be good for her own business, if she was going to take this seriously. Joe, who owned *Bertha*, the beautiful steamboat moored on the opposite promenade, didn't seem to mind, or think her boat's dilapidated state affected his cruises. Joe thought her boat was 'charming' but he may have been exag-gerating slightly for her benefit, she surmised. Luca had been furious for months, telling her how annoying she was at regular intervals – which made her want to paint the boat fluorescent pink! The hull of the boat was sound, as was most of the rest of it, but the paint was peeling here and there. It gave off a shabby-chic vibe that sleek, modern-loving Luca Bowen seemed to hate.

Romy's current view was of Alex and Luca on their boat chatting up a group of smartly dressed women who looked to be around Romy's age of twenty-eight. She picked up her phone as it rang, and was surprised to hear her sister's voice this early in the day. Maya was usually holed up in her art studio most mornings.

'Hey sis,' said Maya breezily and Romy felt her dour mood lift. It was hard to be grumpy with Maya around. She was always smiling these days and who could blame her? She was dating the town's resident movie star! He'd moved in a few years ago and literally bumped into her sister – knocking coffee all over her.

Romy frowned, and wondered if coffee was a theme for their love lives? Her brother Arthur and his girlfriend Daisy had fallen back in love over a coffee by the river, while Romy owned a tearoom that sold coffee. Maybe it would bring her a love story of her own? Then she pulled a grossed-out face, because who needed love? Not her!

'How are you?' she asked her sister, looking around at the boat with fresh eyes. Maybe Luca had a point about tidying it up a bit, she thought.

'I need your help,' said Maya.

Romy frowned. This usually meant some kind of weird scheme or meddling from her family. 'What for?' she asked a touch defensively.

'It's Gran's half-birthday in a month. She wants to keep it small, but she needs a venue.'

Romy grinned at this. 'I've never known anyone else to have quarter or half-birthdays,' she said, shaking her head. Her grandparents had held a half-anniversary party on *Bertha* a few months ago to try and get her brother and

Daisy together. It had worked, but her grandparents would also use the opening of a bag of crisps as an excuse for a party if they could.

'Me neither,' said Maya. Romy could picture her sister rolling her eyes, her shoulder-length brown hair swishing around her shoulders. 'Anyway... Gran wants to hold it on your tea boat. Around fifty people...'

'Fifty people!' Romy could fit about twenty-four seats inside, and probably the same number outside and on the dock – but half of that was uncovered. They had been having lovely weather in the run-up to summer, but you could never make predictions with the British climate. 'She does know I only cater tea, coffee and a few cakes?'

'That's all she wants. She knows you can actually bake, but has offered to buy the cake in. She wants a sit-down cream tea.'

'Cream tea? Oh hell,' sighed Romy, rubbing her achy back from where she'd tried – and failed – to avoid Luca in bed.

Maybe this would give her the push to make a change? Coasting like this wouldn't work in the long term. Romy loved the boat, but hated the mess, if she was honest with herself. She also wanted to make something of the boat, even if it wasn't her original career choice. The ducks needed her protection from the vandals, and she had a soft spot for Bob. Luca would be astounded if she held a successful party there. It could make him back off. Plus hopefully Clara might feel well enough to join them, so it would be good for her too.

'Ok,' she sighed in defeat.

'Ok? Hooray!' shouted Maya and Romy had to hold the phone away from her ear. 'One month from today?'

'A month from today,' Romy agreed, wondering what the hell she'd let herself in for.

'You might need to give the outside of the boat a wash,' said Maya tentatively.

'I know,' Romy agreed. It had been almost two years since she'd found out that Aaron was still married and she finally needed to move on. She still felt humiliation burn in her chest, as well as absolute horror at the pain she'd unwittingly caused his wife.

'I just want the ache to go away,' Romy admitted sorrowfully.

'I know,' soothed her sister. 'But buying a floating teashop and then docking in a prime walking spot might not have been the best plan for a quiet life?'

'I wasn't thinking...'

'I understand. But it is time to consider your future.'

'I don't want to be a vet.'

'But you worked so hard!' Maya protested.

'I don't care,' Romy replied. It was true. 'Everyone knows each other in that industry. They must have heard about what was happening, or known about it before I did.'

'I'm so sorry, Romy. I know you wanted to be a young mum,' said Maya.

'Forget it,' dismissed Romy, although the hurt still filled her body with pain. Her dream of a family with Aaron had never happened, however hard they'd tried, despite all the tests she'd taken. Finally accepting the fact might help her heal. She did worry that it might affect another relationship, but seeing as she was off men anyway, it wasn't really an issue. 'I'll just have to be a cool aunty when you have kids,' she said bravely, brushing the comment away.

Later, she sat jotting down some ideas for the party, then picked a speck of dust off her jeans while she made herself a coffee. She kept trying to ignore her watery eyes. Making Luca eat his words about how awful this place was could be fun, and proving to herself that this business decision was sound would be a bonus.

She looked at her phone, wondering why she hadn't confided in her sister that she'd woken up in the night – reached for Luca – and they'd ended up having mind-blowing and sweaty sex! She hastily shoved the phone back into her jeans pocket and tried not to picture his hand sliding up her leg and his hot mouth capturing hers.

When he'd mentioned finding protection, she'd assured him it wasn't a problem, but perhaps she should have taken more care? Maybe he'd assumed she was on birth control... but then they'd woken up this morning and acted as if nothing had happened, so she wasn't about to bring it up. Her face flamed at how mortified she now was, and how ecstatic he'd made her feel – but repeating one extremely silly mistake was not an option.

Chapter Seven

R omy saw two boots and followed her sightline up two very firm calf muscles. Luca was standing over her as she bent down to take rows of coffee mugs out of her industrial dishwasher. She hated being at a disadvantage to him so she pulled herself up to her full height. He still towered over her and she fumed at this invasion of her personal space, her eyes blazing into his equally fiery ones.

'What do you want?' she asked, stepping into what wasn't a huge kitchen galley space. He'd caught her in the utility area and she was backed up against a counter top. His chest came into contact with hers as he stepped closer, making her breath hitch.

'*Nonna* asked me to check up on you.'

'What? Why?' Romy frowned.

'She texts me every day to check up on you and the house.'

'Me? What does she need to check up on me for? I was moving in to help her.'

'You sure?' he arched an eyebrow at her and she

scowled at him. 'You need to clean the outside of the boat,' he said, throwing his hands up and then placing them on either side of her on the work surface, which brought their faces close together too. For a split second his eyes darkened and their breath meshed together, then he blinked and seemed to realise what he was doing, shaking his head and stepping back. She licked her lips and tried to calm her heartbeat. She wasn't scared of him, but for some reason his presence incensed her, because her pulse was racing as if she'd just run along the dock.

'I like it the way it is,' she said, although that wasn't true. The mess outside annoyed the hell out of her. She enjoyed clean lines, and having the tools of her trade easily accessible. But for some reason she kept the mess around in case he turned up. In a way it proved him right, so she had no idea why she did it. The kitchen was spotless, as were the customer areas. But the boat had seen better days, with its chipped paint and droopy paint-splattered awnings. The floorboards could do with a polish and a few of the outside storage boxes needed fixing. She didn't mention that she'd already ordered new paint, which would be delivered in a few hours. Nor did she say anything about the team she'd booked to come that afternoon and clean the outside of the boat until it shone.

'You should paint the boat, or burn it,' said Luca scathingly, as he ran his hand through his short dark hair and then rubbed his stubbled chin as he gazed around. 'The outside attracts hoodlums and undesirables. Yes, it does!' he added, when she opened her mouth to protest. 'It's dangerous!'

Romy gasped and her fists bunched. She looked directly at him, but he was distracted and was busy running his hands along her coffee machine, which made her shiver.

'This is an amazing bit of kit, though,' he admitted, bending down to take a closer look.

Romy knew he was obsessed with anything electrical and could strip a boat engine before she could blink, it seemed. He'd grown up around boats, as she had, and was often covered in engine grease. She tried really hard not to picture him naked and covered in oil, which was happening more and more lately, especially now that she'd seen him in all his glory.

'Clara loves the fact that the berth is being used again.' Sticking her nose in the air, she shoved him out of her way with her hand on his chest, so she could make a coffee, not at all enjoying the solid feel of muscle under her fingers... She cursed under her breath because more and more, Luca was on her mind and annoying her. Dating hadn't been on her radar for a long while now, but perhaps having him around so often was waking up her libido, and she needed to start thinking about it again?

'*Nonna*'s delusional!' he said, scandalised. 'How can she like seeing this mess from her garden?'

Romy shrugged and tried to ignore him, but he was picking things up and putting them down again and she really wanted to stamp on his toes. 'Can you get out of my space?' she asked, nudging him with her shoulder.

He turned and took hold of her hips with his big paw-like hands, making her yelp. His eyes met hers as they both stilled, and then he let her go.

'Stop doing that or...'

'Or what?' She goaded, but suddenly the air seemed thicker and his eyes darkened again.

'Stop taunting me,' he warned, making Romy frown.

'How am I doing that?' she asked, frustration making her snap.

He brushed a stay lock of hair out of her eyes for a moment and then sighed. Before she could help it, she'd pressed her lips to his and he pushed her back into the counter top and groaned as he deepened the kiss and ground his hips into hers. He tasted like heaven, and she never wanted this to stop. When they broke apart, they were breathless, and Romy's eyes were glazed. What the hell had just happened?

'I need to get back to work,' he said brusquely, as if shaking himself out of a dream. 'I probably shouldn't have come here.'

'Why did you, then?' she shook her head in bewilderment.

'I couldn't keep away,' he said with another quick brush of his lips against hers, whilst picking up the takeout coffee she'd just made for herself because she'd wanted to go for a stroll along the river to try and work out a way to stop thinking of him.

'Hey!' she called after him. 'That was my coffee!'

'So, sue me!' he called over his shoulder with a laugh.

She stomped her feet and then hurried to make a fresh coffee, muttering about ungrateful neighbours and bossy unappreciative men.

Chapter Eight

Clearing up at the end of the day was never Romy's favourite thing. She rubbed her sore back and shooed Bob away from her feet. The last few dog walkers had gone home and she sighed and looked out along the river.

There was barely a breeze. The last rays of the sun glistened across the water, while the swans tucked their heads under their wings for an afternoon snooze. A Taylor Swift song was playing from a speaker somewhere up river and Romy paused to listen to it for a moment.

She liked the fact that people often sat on the grass further along the walkway from her boat. It was sheltered by tall reeds with golden stems and feathery lance-shaped silky heads, and gave a view across the river. They listened to music, played ball games or had occasional barbeques until the warden scooted them off because of the fire hazard.

Boats meandered up and down the river, stopping at various locks along the route. The locks were wide chambers, built across the river, with large gates at either end to hold back the water. The vessels could enter the lock at one level, shut the gates behind them and then the area filled with or emptied out water, until it reached the next level on the river. Romy had got herself a book on the subject when she'd bought the tea boat, although she'd grown up around the river. Of the forty-five non-tidal stretches of the River Thames, around forty of the locks had resident lock keepers, which Romy loved! She adored living on or around the water and thought it must be great for meeting other boat lovers on the river when they stopped at the locks.

Recent visits to Clara had been good. Her hip had been healing well, but then she'd toppled over again, so they'd had to extend her stay.

An uneasy feeling was spreading through Romy's stomach because the past few nights had been heaven. She and Luca had explored each other's bodies, safe in the knowledge that they were now using protection and that he would be going home soon, so they could forget about this whole incident. They still argued incessantly, but weren't quite so uptight, sharing knowing looks and fleeting, sizzling touches. It seemed to be an unspoken rule that they both knew this was transient and that made it even hotter! They couldn't keep their hands off each other at night, but in the morning the distance seeped in and they pretended nothing had happened.

Romy found herself smiling more, though, and the boat looked fit for royalty. Blue and gold awnings made from sails graced the dock, so that customers could relax in the sun or shelter from the rain. Cleaning and repainting the boat had taken a matter of days, and now she wondered why she'd procrastinated for so long. It hadn't been cheap, but admitting that she needed help and borrowing from her sister had been worth it, she felt. She'd had to force herself to ask, because Maya would then know her bank account wasn't exactly filling up at the moment. The joy at annoying Luca had been put aside for the benefit of her business growth. She was fiercely independent, sometimes to her detriment, and hated relying on anyone but herself, but had made an effort to reach out to her sister. Progress!

There was still work to do, but the new Wildlife Tearoom sign, with its gold swirling lettering and illustration of two ducks, courtesy of talented artist Maya, now adorned the side of the boat. The sudden rebrand attracted even more customers who wanted to sit by the river and relax for a while.

Daisy and Arthur had arrived with hedge borders to soften the area too, which Arthur had insisted were a gift. Romy was in awe of what she had created, because the whole site now looked like a professional business with an owner who knew what they were doing. She wondered if this meant that she'd finally decided to stick around and build a base here. Before, she'd seen the boat as a means of escape if things got too heavy being back with her family, but so far, they were leaving her to settle without too much censure about the life she'd left behind. When she'd started the business, she'd often pictured untethering the boat and sailing down river. It had been relentless and lonely, but she hadn't given up. Now she could stand tall and strut to her beautiful tea boat with pride.

She frowned and sniffed the air. Suddenly her stomach was growling and she remembered that the sandwich she'd made for her lunch was still in the fridge. Turning to see Luca walking towards her carrying two covered plates of food, her mouth watered – but at the sight of him, not the food.

'What are you doing here?'

'I thought you might have been too busy to eat lunch, now that your boat is a tourist attraction,' he rolled his eyes. 'It literally took you two days to transform it!' he said with a chuckle. She spluttered a response because he was right.

He had helped her set up all the awnings the night before, after watching in amusement as she'd huffed and puffed while trying to do it alone. He'd intervened just as she was about to blow a gasket and after hours of getting sweaty and panting in the dry evening air, they'd gone inside the darkened tearoom to cool off.

As Luca had stripped off his wet T-shirt, she hadn't been able to take her eyes off him. He'd walked towards her and taken her hand and wordlessly lain her on the tearoom floor, stripping her clothes from her body and kissing every inch of her skin while she'd pulled his slick body to hers and her world had exploded in bliss, leaving her dazed. She'd been like a wild animal that couldn't get enough of his taste or smell as she'd clawed her nails along his skin and urged him closer as he groaned her name. The memory still made her squirm in embarrassment. Her behaviour certainly fitted her new boat theme, she winced.

Before she could say anything else, Luca whipped the covers off the plates he'd been holding, after setting them on one of her tables. 'Madam,' he said, as he held out a chair for her. The evening air was still warm, so she untied her new apron. It had an illustration of two ducks and a swan on the front, beneath the words "Wildlife Tearoom". She sat opposite him, still not quite sure how to behave, so she put her hands in her lap and looked at him under hooded lids.

'I'm a vegetarian,' she said as she sniffed the plate of creamy, peppery, heavenly-smelling spaghetti carbonara.

'I know,' he grinned, nudging the plate nearer to her. 'I added vegan bacon and some broccoli. Is that ok?'

Romy's mouth dropped open in shock that he'd remembered. Aaron still had to be reminded four years on! 'Um… it smells delicious.'

Her stomach rumbled loudly at the scent of the food and he laughed and began expertly turning his fork to fill it with what looked like home-made pasta. The gorgeous Italian could cook from scratch? Why did he have to be so annoying?

'Dig in!' he encouraged, and she didn't need asking twice.

Trying to think of the last time someone other than a family member had cooked her a meal, Romy drew a blank. Aaron liked eating out at fancy restaurants or ordering in from food prep places that did everything but cook the meal, which was where Romy stepped in. She used to love cooking, but now it reminded her of happier times so she'd stopped bothering. Cooking with Luca would be fun, she imagined. It would be messy and hot and probably end up with them making love on the kitchen counter. Her skin shivered at the prospect. Aaron had wanted precision in everything, which was why she always picked up the wonky fruit and vegetables from the supermarket now and enjoyed every bite.

Eating with Luca felt weird, but also strangely normal, and she tried not to overthink the way he was being nice to her now. She was enjoying it more than the sparring, but that was a hard habit to break. She wondered if they would get on as well if they carried on like this, and then bristled as he was clearly ogling her legs while he ate his pasta. She gave him a reproving stare, but he just winked at her and grinned, before scooping another mouthful of pasta between his delectable lips.

Chapter Nine

The sun was coming up and warming Romy's toes as she sat at the little metal table outside Clara's bungalow and enjoyed her breakfast. She crunched on a mouthful of cornflakes and then almost choked as Luca came out of the back door in a pair of grey marl jogging bottoms and nothing else, his chest glistening in the rays of the sun.

Smiling because he didn't notice her at first, he stretched out his glorious muscles from the punishing hours working on the boat. She often saw him scrubbing his boats and fetching and carrying, even though he had loads of staff. The cruise liners took a lot of upkeep, she understood from their evening chats, and she grudgingly admired the astute businessman inside the sexy exterior. However much he acted like a playboy bachelor without a care in the world, Luca spent most of his time looking after his cruise boats, staff and family, it seemed to her. After speaking to his grandmother and parents regularly, he was often on the phone to one of his brothers, sorting out problems, or having a relaxed chat. It was a different side to Luca that she hadn't seen before. He had four more brothers in Italy and they were a big part of his life too. Thanks goodness they didn't all live here, it was overwhelming enough living with Luca and having Alex pop by. Alex teased his brother mercilessly, but Romy thought Luca kind of enjoyed that too and gave as good as he got. She could imagine them causing a ruckus growing up and wondered how their parents had coped with six of them! The idea made Romy feel faint.

Luca turned and caught sight of her and a light of mischief came into his eyes. 'Enjoying the view?'

'Not particularly... or rather, I was until ten minutes ago.' She felt her cheeks flush and cursed under her breath. Why did he always make her feel so cross and pathetic!

She glanced at her phone and jumped up, then remembered that she was still in her pyjama shorts set, because he was suddenly looking at her legs. She glared at him. She refused to blush anymore and this seemed to amuse him, as a slow grin spread across his face.

'We should devise our own morning workout sessions,' he inclined his head towards the yoga mat she'd brought out, intending to do a few stretches after breakfast, and his smile widened.

'In your dreams,' she said, but her lips did quirk up after last night's gymnastics. She pictured his strong hands sliding along her thighs and the sounds she'd made when he'd touched her. He'd almost set her alight with his fingers. They'd expertly strung her out until she'd gasped his name and tipped over the edge of oblivion.

'Frequently...' he quipped, before taking her bowl and coffee cup and wandering back indoors to wash them up for her. She stood in stunned silence. Was he serious? He dreamt about her? What the hell was he playing at? He unnerved her and toyed with her, and she wasn't about to stand for it.

'Look,' she said to his broad, muscled back. She tried to concentrate on how furious she was and not move her eyes down to caress his pert derriere. 'We are living together, it seems, as you won't move out... but cut the pretend flirting, OK? We both enjoy "adult time", so let's leave it at that.'

Her eyes flashed fire at him as he turned to face her. He wasn't smiling now but his eyes held hers and for some reason she felt fear. Not for her safety, but for her heart.

'I wasn't pretending,' he stated clearly, so she wouldn't misunderstand. 'You've always interested me, but you equally annoy the hell out of me, so we are going to have to work out a way to live together that doesn't just result in arguments and hot sex.'

Romy's eyes went wide with shock and she frowned and stepped back, as if to ward off his words. She'd always interested him? What the hell did that mean? And hot sex? Well, she wasn't arguing with that, but now she was picturing him naked and taking hungry possession of her mouth again and that currently took up pretty much all of her day. It was distracting.

'I don't know what to think,' she grumbled. 'Let's try to be friends first and then maybe we'll be fine.'

He nodded and walked past her, but not before she'd caught the scent of his body, fresh out of the shower. It was manly and spicy and she tried to stop herself imagining him soaping himself down with a foaming body wash, water cascading from his broad shoulders. He put the dishes in the sink and before she could think of what to do, he'd grabbed her hand and pulled her with him into the shower, fully clothed, as if he'd been able to read her mind.

'Luca!' she shrieked before his mouth captured hers and

he pinned her hands to her sides and began to kiss his way along the curve of her neck, making her gasp and her back touch the cold shower tiles as the warm water rained down between them. He let her hands go and she immediately began sliding them into his soaking wet joggers and pulling them from his slick skin, over taut, mouth-watering muscles. His eyes met hers for a second and she was shocked by the burning passion in them, before he bent his head to capture her swollen nipple in his mouth as he eased her sodden clothes from her body and let them drop into a pool of water on the floor. His hands cupped her bottom and lifted her up so that her legs could wind around his toned waist and lock behind him, pulling him even closer.

He groaned and kissed her deeply as his hands slipped between them and touched her core, making her gasp his name and throb around his fingers as he took his time exploring every inch of her. He slipped inside her and coherent thought left her, other than the gorgeous man who was currently blowing her mind. Water cascaded around their bodies as they rode each other wildly and then burst into flames as they sank, panting, against the wall.

Chapter Ten

Alex paused by the door to the office and raised an eyebrow. Luca was whistling as he bent his head towards his computer screen, where he was tallying the monthly accounts before sending them to their accountant.

'Someone's happy today,' Alex remarked, slapping his brother playfully on the shoulder.

Luca swung back in his chair and grinned. 'Is that so unusual?'

'Around here, it is. You've been annoying as hell lately.'

Luca frowned and then shrugged. Maybe his brother was right. He'd had a lot on his mind recently. Perhaps he hadn't been as good at hiding it as he'd thought.

'We can't all gallivant around the whole time chatting up women, you know. Some of us have to work.' Luca ducked when Alex threw the tennis ball he'd been holding at his head, and laughed.

Luca liked the fact that they shared this office on the first of their two cruisers. It was quite masculine, Luca supposed, with lots of dark wood, aged leather and metal filing cabinets that were probably fitted when the boat was built. 'Where did you get the ball from?'

'A kid left it on the deck. I didn't want anyone to trip over it.' Alex might be a kid at heart himself, but he was a great business partner who worked just as hard as Luca did.

Luca was forever grateful that Alex had followed him to the U.K and helped him run their *nonno's* business. It had been a hard slog, but they were definitely getting there. 'So, what's with the wide grin?' Alex wanted to know. '*Dimmi* – tell me.'

'Let's just say that I'm glad that *Nonna* asked me to house sit and not you,' was all Luca was prepared to admit.

Alex whistled and then laughed. 'I thought you two hated each other? I was getting ready to step in and stay there instead, but *Nonna* threatened to tan my hide if I did.'

Luca paused in shock. 'What? Why?'

'Because she's been trying to throw you two together for ages. It wouldn't surprise me if she broke her hip on purpose,' Alex grinned.

'You think?' Luca said, horrified.

'No! But I do think she used it to her advantage. She knew exactly what she was doing, forcing you both to stay there.'

'Well, I for one am grateful for that now.'

'I can see that by the stupid grin on your face,' Alex quipped, walking behind Luca to make them both a coffee from the machine on the cabinet behind him. 'I thought you must be off your game because Romy seemed to hate you, my friend.'

'I'm not sure she likes me very much even now,' admitted Luca. 'But I'm working on it,' he winked as his brother handed him his coffee with a smile.

Luca sipped it and closed his eyes in bliss as it hit the

right spot and the room filled with the scent of coffee beans, which reminded him of Romy and kissing her in her little utility room in the Wildlife Tearoom.

'You can't make up excuses to go and moan at her about her boat anymore,' teased his brother, 'because it's becoming a tourist attraction of its own with all those birds. Smart Romy. The marketing is genius. *You* wanted her to get rid of them.'

In Luca's view, Alex was enjoying this a bit too much. 'I just wanted her to tidy the place up. I knew it would be better for her business, but she's just so stubborn.'

Luca had never met another woman who infuriated and turned him on so much at the same time.

'I can think of another person like that,' Alex commented wryly. 'It's no wonder you rile each other up.'

Luca pictured just how annoyed Romy had been when he'd suggested a morning workout, and then recalled the passion she'd engulfed him in when he'd drawn her into the shower. He literally felt like his skin was simmering hot when she was near and he couldn't seem to keep his hands off her now that he'd tasted her skin and kissed her plump lips. He felt like a man obsessed.

His brother knew him too well and punched him lightly on the arm. 'Stop daydreaming, brother. You need to get some work done and then get home early if you want to win this girl and keep *Nonna* happy.'

'I have no idea when *Nonna*'s coming home!' Luca responded. 'I'm enjoying living with Romy, I can't deny, but I do need to get back to the penthouse at some point. I have a beautiful apartment, but I'm living in a tiny cottage.'

'With your dream woman,' Alex pointed out. 'So, get back to work and stop complaining.'

He had a point, Luca decided.

Chapter Eleven

Romy couldn't believe her luck. Her brother, Arthur, and his girlfriend, Daisy, were currently visiting with Daisy's daughter, Brontë. She was hopping from foot to foot in excitement about the boat and the animals.

'You should add further small hedge screening, but in moveable planters,' suggested Daisy. She had designed the outside space for a coffee shop across the water a few months ago and it had been a resounding success. 'It will keep the dogs and ducks off the path and deter break-ins. Add sensor lighting to come on with movement, and you'll worry less about the ducks.'

'Thanks, Daisy,' Romy said.

'If we put the hedges in troughs on wheels and line them along the walkways, then you could probably squeeze in two more tables as well.'

'Great idea. Thank you. Chairs and tables do tend to spill across the walkway from time to time when customers move them.'

The women paused for a moment and Romy watched

her brother wandering around holding Brontë's hand. Romy arched an eyebrow at this and Daisy laughed, but her skin went a bit pink. 'He seems to like spending time with Brontë as much as he does with me,' said Daisy with a smile.

Daisy had moved back from France the previous year, and Maya and Romy had plotted to get their brother and his childhood sweetheart back together. It had been a resounding success, with a few sweat-inducing wobbles in the middle. Romy would hate the same level of meddling in her own life, but it seemed that Clara had taken care of that by throwing Luca her way, anyway. Romy would have never looked at Luca as a potential partner – and she didn't now, she added quickly to her inner monologue. He wasn't as awful as she'd first surmised, though. He was actually quite good company, and he didn't bore her to tears, because he was always arguing with her, or dragging her off to bed. She smiled naughtily at the thought.

'I think Arthur's getting broody,' Romy declared. Daisy's jaw dropped open, before Romy gasped and covered her own mouth. 'Oops.'

'What did I miss?' asked Arthur, as he took in his girl-friend's flushed cheeks and his sister's awkward stance. 'Romy?' he warned. Romy was always speaking first and thinking later.

'We were just discussing Daisy's ideas for the screening,' Romy said, pulling an apologetic face at Daisy. 'Finally, Luca-annoying-Bowen will stop coming round and telling me to clean my site up,' she over-acted, and then cursed under her breath. Her family were like MI5 concerning the smallest white lie. Daisy and Arthur exchanged glances and Romy pouted. 'What?' she asked, then got bored with waiting for an answer and went to serve a customer.

'I think you should have your coffee orders on an app,'

said Arthur, following her. 'I've already looked into it for you. That way, customers can order their coffee while walking and it will be ready for them when they get here. What do you think?'

'You're a genius,' beamed Romy. 'I also want to show you something.' She led them all to the starboard side of the boat, where there was a row of golden hooks with big numbers above them. 'What do you think?' Arthur gave her a puzzled stare and Daisy grinned.

'Brilliant!' said Daisy.

'What is it?' asked Arthur, still frowning.

'It's a drive-through!' laughed Daisy.

'Exactly!' Romy added with glee.

'It looks like a load of hooks to hold garden tools in a shed,' said Arthur in a puzzled tone.

Romy sighed and put her hands on her hips, staring down her brother until he gave in and held his hands up in surrender. 'I'm joking! It looks great. So, boats could order on the app and then come past and pick up their order from the hooks?'

'Exactly. At the moment I've only told a couple of customers, and it might mean queues, but people could get coffee on their trips up and down the river without ever having to leave their boat. They simply pick up the bag with their order inside from the hook with their order number.'

'Unbelievable!' said Arthur, his eyes shining with pride as he scooped his sister under his arm and gave her a big squeeze and ruffled the top of her hair, making it even messier, but she smiled anyway and hugged him back.

'Can you manage all that alone?' asked Daisy. 'I know you wanted a change of scenery, but this is very different to what you studied for.'

'I know,' said Romy, with a genuine smile. 'I was always

stressed and there was so much pressure to make more money. Now I know that was because Aaron was financing his wife's luxurious lifestyle and he was skimming the books. This job, on the other hand, lets me help the local wildlife while earning enough to pay for it all... hopefully. I don't need much.'

Daisy slid her hand around Romy's waist and pulled her close for a hug, but suddenly an image of another hand on her hips and dark eyes boring into hers made Romy gulp. She wondered how annoying Luca would find her drive-through idea.

Romy's mood improved as she imagined more fiery kisses when she riled him up. She gave Daisy a quick hug and then led them all inside the boat with promises of locally famous coffee and the world's biggest teacakes, while she planned what underwear to put on before she told Luca there might be even more boats cruising past his dock!

Chapter Twelve

Romy blew the hair out of her eyes and pinned the duvet to either side of her body with her arms, her heart racing and her body flushed. Luca was lying naked and exhausted next to her. 'I hate the idea,' he sighed.

'I knew you would,' she bit her lip and tried not to laugh, but he pulled the duvet off her as she shrieked in protest and growled as he moved her on top of him. She sat astride him and he caught her breasts in his hands and rubbed her rose-coloured nipples gently with his thumbs, making her sigh with pleasure.

'You enjoy riling me up?' he teased as he raised his hips from the bed and pushed their cores closer together, making her gasp. Romy leaned forward to capture his swollen mouth in hers and he swung her around so that she was beneath him on the bed.

He pinned her hands above her head and then nibbled his way across her collarbone, making her squirm and buck beneath his hips. He pulled away and was serious for a moment. 'What is this?'

'I don't know,' she admitted as she stilled and he rolled off her, taking her with him and scooping her into his side, so she could rest her head on his chest and listen to his beating heart. It was strong and powerful. She took a moment to compose herself, then made a decision. 'I was really hurt by my last partner.'

'What happened?' Luca didn't move or turn to look at her, as if he didn't want to risk her changing her mind about opening up.

'We were together for four years. What he didn't tell me was that he was still married to his wife.' She waited, but didn't experience the dagger-like pain to her heart that she normally felt. She felt Luca draw in a sharp breath and his arms tighten around her.

'I'm sorry, Romy.' He sat up and looked into her eyes, but he seemed tense and she pulled the duvet up to her chin as she settled next to him. She felt vulnerable suddenly, and shivered.

'He had two children and I'd always wanted to start a family young, so we tried for years. I underwent so many tests, but they never found out what the problem was.'

'Did he undergo tests?'

'He already had children,' she frowned. 'What about you? What's your relationship history?'

He paused to think, and then took her hand. 'I've been single for a while. I was in a serious relationship for many years from the age of nineteen, but that broke down.'

He looked away and then reached out for his T-shirt and joggers and pulled them on. His back was slightly hunched and she could see he was in pain. 'Do you still love her?' she asked, a bit terrified of the answer for some reason.

'No,' he scoffed, as he reached out to pull her, fully naked, onto his lap. His eyes roamed her body appreciatively and then he kissed her gently as his hands ran down her arms and then picked up her discarded dressing gown and draped it over her shoulders to keep her warm. 'I got over her a long time ago.'

'What was her name?'

'Bianca.'

'Why did you split up?' she asked quietly, turning to slip her arms around his neck. She'd never felt this comfortable with Aaron and they always went their separate ways after sex. Being with Luca was intimate in a way she wasn't used to. He liked to touch her arm, or leg, or face and kissing seemed to be his favourite pastime these days.

'She cheated on me,' he said simply, and she could see the sadness in his eyes.

'I'm so sorry, Luca. You didn't deserve that.' She kissed his eyes closed, then his jaw and then his mouth.

'You used to think I deserved a whole lot worse, by the fire in your eyes when you looked at me,' he chuckled, brushing her hair out of her eyes and tucking it behind her ear.

'Never that,' she said fiercely. 'No one deserves that.'

He looked deeply into her eyes and gave her a sad smile, then stood up, still holding her in his arms, gently placing her feet on the ground.

'You'll be the undoing of me,' he sighed and before she could say anything else, he'd stolen one last kiss and left her standing in the middle of the bedroom while he went to make them a mug of tea. Her instinct was to follow him, but something about his posture and the sadness in his eyes when he'd mentioned Bianca made her feel that maybe there was more to their story.

Romy knew they needed to go and collect Clara the next day, which would mean big changes for her and Luca.

Would they still see each other if he moved back to his fancy penthouse? That was unknown. She kind of felt that he might care for her, but her man radar hadn't been working for some time and she second-guessed all her choices now.

Once Clara was back, there would be no more sexy bedtimes or showers for two. She wondered if Luca would take the chance to pretend the whole Luca/Romy thing had never happened. Maybe they'd go back to making mean little digs at each other to rile each other up. That had been enjoyable once, because he'd just been the guy from across the water, but now it would hurt.

She vowed to ignore the question marks and make the most of their last night together. Whatever the next day brought, she would deal with it on her own, as always, and she would survive Luca Bowen. It wasn't as if she'd fallen in love...

Chapter Thirteen

Clara was standing at the curb outside the hospital, dressed in dark green leggings, a flowy white blouse and a long cardigan. She looked very elegant for someone who had recently had surgery. Next to her was a distinguished looking gentleman with a neat grey beard and a jaunty hat. Luca turned to Romy, as if she would know what was going on, but she shrugged.

'I'm going to Henry's holiday cottage to recuperate,' Clara stated as they approached. Before Luca could protest, she added, 'My doctor says the sea is soothing and Henry has a place right by it.'

'Nice to meet you, Henry,' said Romy, reaching in to shake his hand. She could clearly feel Luca about to erupt so her other hand went to him and she briefly touched his arm to keep him cool. He looked at her hand for a moment attempting to rein in his temper.

'But you live by the river!' he burst out and Romy rolled her eyes.

'Well, that didn't work,' Romy muttered under her breath, but he heard her.

'I need calm,' Clara shared a look with her friend Henry, and Romy frowned.

'So... you're not coming back to the bungalow?' Romy clarified, a mix of emotions swirling around them all.

'Not for a little while,' said Clara, with a nod to Henry to put her bag in his car, which was parked across the road.

'Won't you need more clothes?' Romy frowned at her small bag, mostly full of the nightshirts she had been wearing recently.

'I can buy clothes,' Clara brushed off that concern. 'There's a sweet little town just a short walk away from Henry's place.' Luca was bursting to ask how she knew this, as he had never met Henry before. 'I feel so much more relaxed knowing you are both looking after my home.'

'Both?' asked Luca in horror. 'I have my own flat!'

Romy winced and he cursed under his breath at his thoughtless words. He'd been torn between looking forward to moving back to his huge relaxing flat, and dreading it. Romy didn't seem happy either, and that stung. Luca's heart hardened. 'But *Nonna—*' he protested.

'Don't "*Nonna*" me,' she scolded and Luca's skin tinged red. Romy looked at him and seemed to find the exchange fascinating. 'I know you have a fancy flat, but I'm family and I need your help. Romy is doing her bit.'

'Am I?' she asked with a frown and then she quickly changed tack at Clara's stern look. 'I am,' she said firmly as she smiled sweetly at Luca.

'So, you need to do your duty. Surely it gives you more time to rest, without the commute through the rush hour every day?' she said pointedly.

Romy spoke up. 'I think Clara is trying to get you to ease up on your workload,' she suggested gently.

Travelling did take hours out of his day, and it was

easier to simply walk across the bridge and relax after work, even though being around Romy wasn't that relaxing. He was always thinking of ways to seduce her without her realising what he was doing. Sometimes he was subtle, often blatant, but that was because she always ignored his signals until her threw her over his shoulder or dragged her into the shower. It wasn't ideal for his ego.

'You could always sublet your flat.' Clara winked at Romy and she smothered a laugh.

'What?' he stepped back in shock. 'Exactly how long are you going to the coast for?'

Luca gave Romy a look, pleading for her to help him out, and she caved. 'Maybe a few days will be enough, and perhaps it might be nice if we were formally introduced to Henry,' she suggested with a look over her shoulder at Clara's friend. He seemed to be about Clara's own age and already had the car door open for a fast getaway.

'My doctor suggested eight weeks,' Clara responded quickly as she moved towards the car.

'Two months!' Luca stepped into her path and caught her arm gently.

'He can add up,' Romy mumbled under her breath and he gave her a scathing look. 'Don't worry. I'll be spending a lot of time on the boat and you'll pretty much have the place to yourself,' she went on.

Luca's head whipped round and he winced. 'That's not what I meant, Romy.'

Clara held her hand up to prevent further chat. 'I need a quiet word with my grandson. Henry is an old friend from my youth, we meet up whenever he's in Windsor. You don't need to worry that he's a serial killer,' she laughed suddenly.

Romy chuckled, but then darted one last look at Henry to make sure. 'I'll go and get us a coffee and meet you back at your car,' she told Luca who scowled, so she gave him a warning look.

Clara's health was paramount, so he'd just have to suck it up, however much he was scared of living with Romy because he already feared for his heart.

'What the hell are you thinking?' he asked Clara as they watched Romy walk away.

'I'm thinking it's about time you stopped messing about and actually took that girl to dinner,' she scolded. He gulped, trying not to picture Romy laying naked in their bed after he'd cooked her spaghetti carbonara.

'She told me you never mentioned we were related, and hid all the family photos before she came to visit your place?' he protested.

Clara sighed and patted his hand. 'You both seemed to enjoy fighting a bit too much. I didn't want to scare her off before I had a chance to knock your silly heads together!'

'What do you mean?'

'You've been avoiding relationships for too long, Luca. You can't keep using what happened with Bianca as an excuse to push everyone away. You and Romy would be perfect together and I already think of her as my grand-daughter.'

'You can't pick who I date!' he admonished, throwing his hands up into the air.

'You don't date anyone suitable,' she tutted.

He shook his head. His grandmother had never meddled in his love life before... except maybe once.

'Who the hell is this Henry?' he asked in exasperation.

'He's an old friend. We chat on the phone, but he's been popping in to visit me in hospital and suggested his place to recuperate.'

Luca raised an eyebrow at this, and said, 'I bet he did...'

Clara laughed and swatted his arm playfully. 'I'm old enough to know what I'm doing.'

'And I'm not?'

'Clearly,' she answered and then chuckled, which made him smile. She pulled him in for a warm hug and rested her face on his chest like Romy sometimes did. 'Have your feelings for her changed?'

'What feelings?'

'The ones that you've always had for Romy. Do you think I'm an idiot?'

Luca scratched his head and ignored the comment for a moment, his eyes focusing in on his grandmother. She was now smiling sweetly and waving at Henry, to come and help her to the car.

'Don't mess this up,' she told Luca firmly.

He sighed and his shoulders drooped. 'I'll try not to,' he said, and she lifted his chin with her hand.

'You deserve to be loved, and so does Romy,' she said as she took Henry's arm and let him lead her to the car.

Luca stared after her and felt like he'd been run over with a truck. His grandmother was right. He was in love with Romy Lopez.

Chapter Fourteen

Luca pulled into a restaurant car park as they got nearer town and turned off the engine. 'Dinner?'

'Good idea. Clara was right about you looking tired.'

'Thanks,' he laughed and she flushed.

'You know what I mean,' she chided.

'My flatmate is insatiable,' he teased and she went an even brighter shade of red and batted his hand away when he tried to capture it in his.

He caught her face in his hand for a second and gave her a fleeting kiss on the lips after brushing her hair out of her eyes, which was something he loved to do, so that he could see her face clearly. She used her hair as a shield, he'd worked out, and he never wanted her to feel the need to hide her emotions from him. It had felt good to face his grandmother with someone by his side, even if they were uncertain of their connection right now. He'd understood that Romy would be there for him, even if he annoyed the hell out of her still. What she didn't know was that his heart was already in her hands, which made it even more difficult to open up to her, in case she ran away.

They walked up to the Italian restaurant he'd parked in front of. It was still early, so there weren't many people about, but the sky was becoming darker and a couple of stars could be seen twinkling. He slipped his hand into hers as they reached the door to the brick building with ornate wooden windows, and she didn't pull away this time.

They'd become much closer since they'd spoken about their ex-partners, but there was still so much more he had to say. She'd been so open when she'd said she didn't think she could have children, and it had held him back from talking about Bianca. There was still a whole mess of emotions tied up with that situation and Bianca's brutal treatment of him and her blatant disregard for his feelings had scarred him inside. Romy was becoming more and more important to him, but he wasn't sure how to mesh the old with the new without ruining the tenuous relationship he was trying to build.

His own experience had made him feel like his heart was being wrenched from his chest and he still hadn't found a way out of the pain, even years later. Opening up to Romy was something he wanted to do, but speaking up cut open old wounds and he wasn't sure if this was just something casual to her. It was a thought he hated, but his *nonna* was right about possibly scaring her away. Romy clearly wasn't over her own ex and Luca didn't know if he had the strength to trust himself in a relationship again.

They were led to a table in the corner that had low lighting. The dark green walls and simple white linen place settings gave a feeling of intimacy. He appreciated the small vase of plump roses on the table, with dark pink petals and a warm musk scent. They chose a pizza each and shared a crisp mixed salad with green olives drizzled with balsamic vinegar and olive oil. They picked up their pizzas with their fingers and Luca was mesmerised for a moment when Romy caught a bit of meting cheese in her mouth and licked her fingers afterwards, making him salivate – and not for the food. What was it with this woman and his libido?

'I've been trying to keep up with Alex's plans to expand further up the river,' he said, trying to find a neutral topic. 'There's a company selling two boats. It's a bit of a headache to sort out all the potential upgrades they will need. Staffing and basic refits would be the first tasks. *Nonna* being unwell at the same time...' He rubbed his hands through his hair and Romy put her hand on his arm in comfort.

'Plus, you being asked to babysit the new lodger?' she asked and then watched as a secret smile unfurled on his face and the same mischief that lit Clara's eyes filled his.

'*Nonna* knows exactly what she'd doing.'

'What do you mean?'

'I guess I've spoken about how much you annoy me, too many times.'

'I'm confused.'

'She thinks I like you and she's throwing us together. That would be my conclusion.'

'I did wonder why. Maybe I spoke about you a bit too much too?' she admitted, her eyes sparkling

He had to resist the urge to pull her across the table and kiss her, so he picked up her hand and kissed the soft skin of her wrist instead.

Happiness radiated through him that she'd maybe felt the same way he did – but it could just be wishful thinking, he reasoned. He was exhausted and the buyout was clearly taking its toll. He just wasn't used to having anyone else around to notice.

'I like the idea of you talking about me, or thinking of me,' he admitted, finding a perfect olive and offering it to her. She smiled and bit into it, leaving the other half for him to pop into his mouth. 'Maybe there is some truth in *Nonna*'s theory,' he sighed, rubbing his neck.

'But you're always telling me how annoying I am.'

'You are annoying,' he grinned, his hand taking hers again and turning it palm up on the table so that he could trail his finger along her pulse, making it jump – but she didn't take her hand away.

'Eat up,' he urged, changing the subject. 'Your boat looks amazing now,' he admitted and she grinned, which made his heart soar. 'You need your strength to keep up with all the work you've been doing, too.'

'Plus our midnight gymnastics,' she bit her lip in mirth. He loved how she was forward at times, and then shy at others.

'That definitely wears me out,' he laughed as she grinned. 'I'm not sure I ever want to stop, though,' he added, and she gulped and became suddenly very interested in her pizza.

Chapter Fifteen

The Wildlife Tearoom was resplendent, with its duck egg blue paint freshly washed, and gold bunting reaching from the dock. It was the weekend, but Romy had closed early to get ready for her grandmother's half-birthday.

For the first time in a while, Romy had visited the hairdressers, at Maya's insistence, and her hair was a glossy waterfall around her face. She was wearing one of the dresses she used to wear when she was dating Aaron. It had tiny spaghetti straps that tied in bows on her shoulders, a fitted bodice and a skirt that stopped at mid calf, giving a glimpse of toned leg. It clung to her chest in all the right places and she used to feel like a million dollars in it. Now she felt a bit exposed. Things with Luca had been heating up over the past month and she was finally letting down walls and enjoying his company, but he'd never seen her like this.

Then Luca walked in and whistled in appreciation, and she felt her skin warm up. He took her hand and twirled her around, giving him a further glimpse of her legs. He pulled her into his chest to wrap his arms around her and kissed her until her lips were plump and glossy, her skin tingling as his fingers skimmed her backside. What was it with this man? She'd spent the past few days feeling sick with nerves about the party but whenever she was with him lately she felt light-headed.

He released her after stealing one more kiss and she touched her lips, knowing she'd have to refresh her lipstick, but not really caring. He leaned on the kitchen counter and watched her as she looked around for her handbag. She'd spent a few days prepping the cream tea, making scones and dolloping thick cream into delicate little pots for each table. Adding homemade strawberry jam was the final touch. Her grandmother had dropped the jam round the night before, staying for a cup of tea and a natter, or inquisition, Luca had laughed afterwards. They'd both had to have a glass of wine to recover, but Romy's stomach still hadn't settled and she'd thrown hers away.

The tables on the boat had been laid with soft blue linens and Maya's florist friend Leah had brought round garland strings to hang across the ceiling and posies to attach to each chair. Maya had found little teapot-shaped favour boxes that they had filled with mouth-watering chocolate delicacies of salted caramel truffles, white chocolate raspberry filled stars and milk chocolate covered coconut creams, and placed one box at each table setting. Romy had sat down the previous evening and taken in the fact that this was now her business. She could rent the space out to parties and make quite a lot of money.

The new wildlife angle seemed to bring people in droves, hoping to see the birds by the river at close hand. A few more tables had been added inside and the deck looked really smart. She could see herself paying Maya's loan back quite quickly, and her new association with the swan sanctuary helped them both. Romy handed out leaflets about the work of the sanctuary, to make people more aware of looking after the wildlife on the river. Donations were up and in return, they had a bunch of leaflets and a poster about the Wildlife Tearoom that they showcased in their reception area. It helped Romy that she could take injured birds to the sanctuary and she was happy to assist them with the upkeep and health checks on the swans on a volunteer basis when she could.

'Are you ok?' she asked him, that swirly feeling in her stomach again.

'I wondered exactly what this is?'

'This?'

'Us.'

'Us?'

'Romy, are you just going to keep repeating everything I say?' he teased, taking her hand and pulling her closer.

'Um... I don't know. I thought you wanted to keep it a secret?'

'I don't,' he answered, and she reeled back in shock. '*Nonna* clearly already knows,' he said, which made Romy's lips creep up into a smile.

'She's quite manipulative, it turns out,' she laughed, trying to ease the tension in her back by rubbing it with the base of her other hand.

'She is, but I'm kind of glad about that now,' he admitted, his eyes not leaving hers.

'You are?' she gulped as his free hand caught her hip and then slipped lower to cup her backside and pull their hips together.

'I am,' he confirmed, kissing her lips gently. 'Are you?'

She could sense her next answer was important to him. 'Um... Yes. I am.'

'Are you sure?' he frowned, and his hands slipped from hers, moving to sit on a stool by the breakfast bar.

'Of course!' she reassured, but the wobble in her voice belied her.

'We act like a couple,' said Luca.

'We do?' she frowned.

'Romy. We live together, sometimes work together, eat together and make love together!'

Her eyes bugged out at his honesty, but then he'd never been one for even the smallest lie. This was getting serious, though, and her dodgy stomach was back. She wanted to run to the toilet to be sick, but took a calming breath instead.

'Look,' she said. 'Let's talk about this tomorrow.'

'I think we should tell our families. A lot of them will be at the party tonight.'

Romy's jaw dropped open, but then her phone buzzed with a text. They both turned to look at where she'd left it on the countertop. They stared at the screen as a message from Aaron popped up saying he missed her and wanted to meet up. Luca looked at her and then the phone and then got up to let her answer the message privately, but she caught his arm.

'That is definitely not what I want... ever.' She said vehemently.

'Are you sure?'

'I've never been surer of anything in my life.' She took his hand and made him sit down again 'You've made me see what a relationship is. I don't even know if this is a relationship, but it's better than anything I ever had with Aaron,' she admitted and he sighed and pulled her into his arms.

She rested her cheek against his chest, her favourite place, and slid her hands down to his pert derriere with a grin. He smiled and caught her hand.

'No time for that,' he laughed. 'But we are definitely a couple,' he said, and she leaned in and kissed him. 'Come on. Your grandmother's half-birthday can't start late because I want to send them all home and spend the evening ravishing you!'

'I love that idea,' she said happily as she started balancing box after box of cakes in her arms.

'Woah,' he said, as he took a few of them. 'We need sustenance to build up our energy for later, so no dropping the cakes,' he joked.

Maya stuck her head around the door as they tried to carry everything and rushed in to help. Her partner Noah was behind her and Romy asked him to grab her bag and jumper for later when the air began to get cool.

Music was already playing as they stepped outside and pride swelled in Romy's chest as she looked at her business. The whole top of the boat now had a waterproof layer, with plants and nesting boxes dotted along it. The mallard ducks were mainly inhabiting the roof, but an elegant mute swan, owned by the monarchy, was toddling along the bow before he flew back into the river. The tradition of scooping both adults and cygnets from the water in the annual Swan Upping census, to weigh and tag them on the leg, was roughly nine hundred years old. Romy had learned more about this part of local wildlife conservation on her visits to the swan sanctuary.

She loved how resilient and adaptable the ducks were, too. Some had up to twelve chicks following them around. The black-headed gulls also stopped by, and there was a family of moorhens that often rustled in the undergrowth by the riverbank and visited the café when it was closed, for scraps dropped on the floor. Two Egyptian geese seemed to have taken a shine to her roof. It was starting to get a bit crowded!

People began walking over the bridge from the village and she saw Arthur strolling along with their grandparents and waved. She rushed forward to get the last batch of cakes from inside and then turned to survey her domain. Maya followed to help her with the coffee machine and the urn that kept her water hot for the gallons of tea she sold every day.

Maya looked across to Noah and Luca who were laughing over something Noah had said. Noah slapped him heartily on the back and they both looked their way, so the girls busied themselves and pretended not to notice.

'What is going on with you and Luca?' hissed Maya under her breath.

'What do you mean?' Romy asked, but her stomach was tied up in knots.

'It's written all over your faces!' her sister crowed. Romy flushed. Luca was already welcoming everyone and Maya's eyes narrowed as she nudged her sister in the ribs. 'When did Luca Bowen become so at home on this boat?'

'After we made love on the tearoom floor!' Romy laughed and then covered her mouth in shock as Maya's eyes sparkled in delight and then she grabbed her sister in a tight hug, almost breaking her ribs.

'At last!'

'What do you mean, at last?' She frowned, looking at Luca and trying to stop her heart melting.

'You two have been dancing around each other for ever.'

'We have?'

Maya rolled her eyes and patted her sister's back in sympathy.

'I'm scared,' admitted Romy.

'Don't be! Just let yourself enjoy the moment for once, without second guessing your decisions. You know what you're doing.'

Then their conversation was cut short by the arrival of the half-birthday girl. Maya rushed forward to greet her grandparents and the other guests, but the first thing she did was raise an eyebrow to Romy about Luca, who was now standing by her side.

'Happy half-birthday!' said Romy, as a distraction and ushered them all inside, her cheeks warm and her heart full of promise as Luca slipped his hand into hers and gave it a squeeze of solidarity.

Chapter Sixteen

'The party has been a such a success!' Maya said, hugging her sister as they led everyone outside. The group was eclectic, with lots of colourful attire – no surprise when Ettie threw impromptu parties with unusual themes. The last one was a glitter party with glow in the dark icing on bright pink cupcakes. Goodness knows what had been in them to make them so bright, Romy mused, knowing it could well be an exotic spice or natural colouring from her grandad's huge glasshouse full of plants. Ettie's only stipulation for today had been about fun, so everyone had risen to the occasion, in outfits featuring lots of different colours and textures including a pink suit with flamingos tumbling all over it. One man was wearing a crown, and Romy had no idea if it was real or fake.

Luca had been introduced to everyone as her partner and it had felt good to enjoy the hugs of congratulations from friends and family, most of whom weren't even surprised. People were milling around and saying their goodbyes when Romy noticed a beautiful woman with long dark hair staring at the group from the middle of the bridge that led up to town. Luca froze beside her as the young boy with her spotted them too and called out. '*Papà!*' he said with excitement, as he broke free from his mother and ran towards Luca with open arms. Luca bent down to swing him into his arms and hug him closely. The child looked to be around eight or ten and Luca turned to her with sorrowful eyes and mumbled that he needed to speak to Bianca. Bianca? *Papà?* What the hell?

Romy froze and then turned to Maya, but she seemed just as stunned, with an appalled look on her face. They both fixed their gaze on Alex. He was doing his best to avoid them by ducking behind the crowd, who were now all focussed on Luca and the child, who was walking along holding his hand.

'Well?' Maya demanded of Alex, her eyes flashing fire and her hands on her hips.

'Um,' he winced, holding his hands up in defence as if to ward off what he clearly knew was coming. 'That's Luca's wife, Bianca, and his son, Matteo.' The colour drained from Romy's face and she had to grab onto Maya for support. Maya put her arm around her sister and hugged her to her side. 'They met in Italy.'

'You have got to be kidding me?' raged Maya. 'He's just spent the past two hours being introduced to our family as Romy's partner.'

Alex looked pained and turned to watch his brother. Luca's posture was rigid and he didn't look happy. Bianca, on the other hand, was beaming from ear to ear as she leaned in and kissed Luca on each cheek.

'Did you know about this?' Maya asked her sister, concern in her voice.

'What do you think?' cried Romy. 'It's happening again.' She pushed past everyone and fled into the bungalow, while

Maya quickly spoke to the last few guests and said goodbye in the hope they would all go home.

Romy ran to the bathroom and promptly threw up the contents of her stomach, then slid to the floor and let the tears flow. Her body was racked with sobs as she ran through the number of opportunities Luca had had to tell her he was married! That he had a child! She'd opened her heart and confided in him about not being able to have a baby and he hadn't bothered to mention that he already had a child. He was the one who had pushed her to tell everyone they were a couple, and now she'd been humiliated again. He'd left without a backward glance, probably because he'd been caught out in front of everyone. Tears spilled out of her eyes. Looking up, hearing Maya tentatively opening the door, she hiccoughed and tried to stem the tears, but they continued to flow.

'Are they all here?' she asked, knowing they would be.

Maya nodded, handing her a wodge of tissue paper to dab her eyes. 'Grandad is making tea and Gran is looking for whiskey to add to it. Daisy took Brontë home, but Noah and Arthur are in the lounge.'

Romy put her head in her hands. All the little remaining energy flowed out of her and her shoulders sagged in defeat. Maya looked like she wanted to say something else, so Romy sighed. 'Out with it.'

'Clara has just got back, too. She was supposed to be here for the party, but got caught in traffic.'

'Oh, bloody hell,' Romy cried. 'I can't face any of them.'

'You have to. You haven't done anything wrong.'

'He's a married man,' shouted Romy, jumping up and bunching her fists. Luca had clearly left with his family, as he wasn't here, but she really wanted to punch him where it hurt.

The door opened a fraction and Ettie poked her head around the door. She was wearing a feathered headpiece, so it arrived before her face did and gave the game away. 'Come and have some whiskey. It's good for shock.'

'I have appalling taste in men,' cried Romy.

Maya took her hand, but didn't disagree.

'It seems Luca has gone back to his flat,' said Ettie, her tone suggesting good riddance.

'At least you don't have to speak to him again,' said Maya.

'I'm living in his grandmother's bungalow!' said Romy. 'I need to get out.' She pushed past her grandmother, but then came face to face with Clara, whose forehead was creased with worry.

'I'm so sorry, Romy. We need to chat,' she said, leading Romy past her family and out to the metal chair and table set, where two steaming cups of tea and two hefty whiskey filled glasses had been placed.

Romy picked up the whiskey but even the smell turned her stomach, so she hastily put it down again. Her eyes were red and sore from crying and humiliation burned in her soul. The day had begun with such happiness and so many possibilities for the future, and now she was back to square one. Weirdly, she felt even more crushed than she had when she'd found out about Aaron's lies.

Clara took her hand across the table and Romy tried not to flinch. 'Will you give me a moment to explain?'

Chapter Seventeen

Romy put her hands into her lap. Pain sliced through her stomach, but she refused to give in to it and stayed rigid against the back of the chair. She had been betrayed by friends before, so this was nothing new. 'How could you let me get mixed up in this? I thought you were my friend?'

Tears filled Clara's eyes and she wiped them away. 'I am your friend, Romy.'

'Is that why you hid photos of Luca and Alex when I came round? Were they with Matteo and Bianca?' she almost spat out.

'It wasn't like that,' said Clara calmly with a deep sigh. 'I could see how Luca's eyes followed you around and I thought perhaps you might like him too.'

When Romy didn't answer, she continued. 'You didn't come in very often and I didn't want to scare you off if you thought we were related. I knew you thought you hated him, but I guessed that emotion might have been misplaced. He's a wonderful man and you deserve that.'

'Wonderful?' scoffed Romy, throwing her hands into the

air, almost knocking the whiskey over. She could see her family out of the corner of her eye, huddled in the lounge, waiting for her to return. She'd let them down, again.

'I assumed he'd tell you about Matteo and Bianca when you began to trust each other. I gathered you'd had a tough time too, so I thought you could bring happiness into each other's lives. Does it matter so much that he has a child?'

'A child?' Scoffed Romy. 'It isn't about the fact that he didn't tell me he is a father, after I told him I didn't think I could conceive...' Clara gasped and covered her mouth, her eyes going glassy with unshed tears. 'But my last partner told me he was single, and he was married, too.'

'Oh Romy,' Clara took her hand again. 'I didn't realise. You and Luca are more alike that I realised.'

'I'm not married!'

'Neither is he.'

Romy frowned and sat back in her chair. 'What do you mean? Alex just told us that Bianca was his wife.'

Clara closed her eyes for a moment and then leaned her elbows on the table, making Romy worry the stress was too much for her, so she tried to calm down... but it was impossible. She wanted to wail and scream and smash things.

'Bianca *was* Luca's wife. They dated straight from school in Italy and by the age of twenty-one, she was pregnant.' Romy felt like she'd been punched in the guts, and couldn't speak. 'Luca of course stood by her, even though she was difficult to live with. She's always been volatile and self-centred, but this took the biscuit.' Clara's eyes darkened and her jaw set. It was Romy's turn to be confused.

'I don't understand.'

Clara seemed to be deciding how honest to be, but then sat back too and looked at Romy. Romy could see this conversation wasn't easy for her either. 'She was unfaithful.

The other guy didn't want his child, so she told Luca the baby was his.' Clara sniffed and took a sip of her tea, then picked up the whiskey and took a hefty slug. Romy couldn't believe what she was hearing.

'He married her and looked after the child. Then a few years ago, when Matteo was five, the biological father decided he wanted to claim his son, win Bianca back and bring his son to England, which was pathetically easy. She jumped at the chance, even after he'd deserted her in a time of need. She then had to tell Luca the truth.'

Romy gasped and she held onto her heart. Fresh tears sprang to her eyes and seeped down her cheeks.

'Oh my God.'

'We couldn't believe someone could treat another human being that way. I've never seen a man so broken. He wasn't in love with Bianca by then, but he loved his child.'

Romy brushed her tears away and moved her chair closer to give Clara a hug. 'I'm so sorry. I can't believe it.'

'It's probably why Luca hadn't told you yet. I'm sure he would have in time, but if you told him you'd tried for children and he said he had a son... well, perhaps he was waiting for the right moment.'

'To say he's married with a child?'

'He's been divorced for years, and she tricked him into marriage. It breaks him to talk about it.'

'How can he even look at her?'

'She's the mother of his child,' Clara said simply. 'Matteo might not be Luca's biological child, but he's still his son.'

'They meet regularly?'

'Not as often as Luca would like, but Bianca did one thing right and didn't stop them seeing each other. Matteo was broken by this too. As far as he's concerned now, he has two fathers. We are still his family.'

'How did Luca cope?'

'He came here with his brother and joined his grandfather's business. He carried a lot of grief and shut away the part of himself that could love somebody, to protect himself. You changed that.'

Romy put her face in her hands. Her mind was whizzing back and forth through every conversation she'd had with Luca, as she tried to think if this was another fling, or if it could lead to love. She herself had closed off her heart to protect it, so maybe she'd only been living a half-life too. The thought stung.

'Did he know Matteo was arriving today?'

'No. Bianca doesn't like plans. It's hard for Luca to see his son, and then she turns up out of the blue. Obviously, Luca spent years thinking Matteo was his biological son, and they lived together before Bianca left, so it's doubly hard. The only way he could cope was moving here too. I'm not sure how much it has helped, but at least he can still see his son. We were already here, and having us nearby has helped, I hope.'

'Poor Luca,' sighed Romy sadly, her bones feeling like lead. 'He could have told me.'

'I know,' was all Clara said as they got up. They held hands while they stepped back inside.

Chapter Eighteen

Luca settled his son at his desk with a computer game on his laptop and motioned for Bianca to join him out on the balcony of his penthouse flat. He looked around at the masculine décor, deep blues and grey tones, minimal fuss, and kind of missed the soft comfort of his grandmother's bungalow. He didn't have trinkets or photo frames reminding him of memories. It made him realise how fleeting his relationships had been before he met Romy and that his *nonna* had been right. His work had consumed his life.

'Why are you here?' he asked Bianca.

She responded with the high tinkly laugh that had always grated on his nerves. 'Aren't you pleased to see us?'

'I'm always glad to see my son,' he ground out.

'Guiseppe had some meetings in London, so we popped over to see you. He leaves me alone too much and I get bored.'

'They don't have things to do in Oxford? Beautiful architecture, botanical gardens, the Bodleian library... the prison,' he added under his breath, as she'd taken half his inheritance from his grandfather when she'd left, though she knew the whole marriage had been a sham. 'You didn't think to let me know so I could make plans with Matteo?'

He closed his eyes and tried to stay calm, but it was ridiculously difficult with his ex. He always remembered the phrase, "you can't reason with the unreasonable", when he saw her. Nothing much she said made sense, or maybe he just believed little of it anyway.

'You saw him in Italy a few months ago when we visited our parents. I knew you'd make time for us. You always do,' she purred and tried to slide her arms around his waist, but he moved away.

'How is Matteo doing in school?'

'Oh pfft! We talk about this endlessly. You know he's ok.'

'He doesn't like the private school Guiseppe has moved him to. You're aware of that.'

'He's getting used to it.'

When he gave her a stern stare, she threw her hands up in exasperation.

'Ask him!'

'How long are you here for?'

'Just a few days... maybe a week.'

Luca tried to hold onto his temper. Things had been perfect at the party and Romy's family seemed to have welcomed him with open arms. Even Arthur, who wasn't shy with opinions on men his sisters dated, had slapped him on the back and handed him a beer. Now he'd want to throttle him!

He should have told Romy about his past, but it still almost killed him that the beautiful boy in the other room wasn't his biological son, though Luca would lay down his life for that child. Biology didn't change the fact that Matteo was his, or how he felt about him, but it brought a world of fear about Matteo being taken away from him and other people making decisions in his life.

Luca had been dealing with this for years now, and the suffering didn't stop with Bianca's flighty ways. It was emotionally draining, and he had little energy for much else. Hence the faceless flat in the middle of town and the appeal of quick and undemanding relationships. Bianca had made his life hell for years with her high expectations and demands, before she'd blurted out that she was running off to live with the real father of their son, carelessly waving the paternity test result envelope in his face, so he'd had to turn away, in case she saw him cry. He could barely look at her at times, but he had no choice, for the wellbeing of Matteo.

Romy telling him she couldn't have children hadn't scared him away, because he was already a father and she was enough for any man, but he should have confided in her in that moment and now she probably hated him. He hadn't even had a chance to call her, or send her a text to apologise, because his time with his son was so precious. He quickly reached for his phone and opened up a fresh text.

'What were you doing with that group by the dock, and why was the boat covered in ducks?' Bianca broke into his thoughts.

Luca sighed and shut his phone down again.

'It was a birthday party and it's called the Wildlife Tearoom. The ducks live there,' he explained.

He tried not to picture capturing Romy's face during the party while they were cleaning up in the kitchen and stealing a kiss, which had held so much promise for later. Now he didn't know if he'd ever kiss her again and it felt like a sucker punch to the ribs and a sharp dagger in his heart.

'Maybe we can take Matteo to see the birds?' Bianca said casually and his eyes narrowed.

She always tried to cause as much trouble as possible, so he bet his parents had already told her about the party. They still saw Matteo regularly when they visited and tried to be civil to the woman who had broken their son's heart when they video-called Matteo.

'I'm starving,' she said grumpily when he didn't answer. She stalked over to his sleek black granite kitchen area and began opening cupboards and shutting them again. 'There's no food here.' He wasn't about to say he'd been living at Clara's bungalow because he'd never hear the end of the questions. 'You could take us out to dinner,' she suggested.

'How about Matteo and I go out for dinner?' he sighed as he joined her in the kitchen. 'I can drop you back at the hotel with your husband and I can spend some time with my son.'

'Can we?' asked Matteo, jumping up from his seat, his eyes shining. Luca ruffled the top of his dark hair, so like his own. He slipped an arm around his son's shoulders, his heart melting at the sight of him. Seeing him was hard, but being apart was harder. Now that Matteo lived with Guiseppe and Bianca in a huge mansion in Oxford, the boy's life was busier than ever. Luca still visited him every month and spoke to him daily, but it was never enough. He sometimes felt like his son was slipping through his fingers, but there was nothing he could do about it.

Chapter 19

Romy pulled the covers over her head and tried to block out the world. She hated being in the bed without Luca, and Clara was tiptoeing around her. They'd spent the night before sitting up late and talking about both of their families, but Romy's heart was still broken. She knew it must be incredibly hard for Luca to trust anyone now, but she'd also thought they were beginning to open up with each other. It turned out she was doing that, and he was keeping secrets.

She groaned and pushed the covers back, swinging her legs to the side of the bed and forcing herself to get up. Every part of her body ached, but she guessed that was from the emotional turmoil. Her breasts were sore and she'd got up to wee three times in the night, which was making her even grumpier through lack of sleep.

She took her time over her morning shower and then headed towards her tea boat, glad for once that Clara was still sleeping. Romy's emotions were wrung out and she felt that someone could literally look at her the wrong way and she'd burst into floods of tears.

She unlocked the door and rubbed her back. The detritus of the party had been cleaned away and she sent up a prayer of thanks for her sister, as she knew Maya would have been the one sweeping the floors while worrying about her. She began turning things on and the hum of the coffee machine soothed her. She'd gone off coffee a bit lately, which was unheard of, so she was determined to try a few sips today. She refused to let Luca ruin everything for her. Some of the old animosity she'd felt for him was simmering under the surface.

Her phone beeped and she grabbed it, hoping to see something from Luca, but it was another text from Aaron. She angrily swiped to delete it but brought the message up by mistake. The phone rang, making her jump, and she looked at the screen first before answering.

'What do you want?' she asked, her temper getting shorter.

'I want to speak to you, Romy,' said Aaron. 'I've sent you so many texts. You don't reply.'

'Uh, don't you think that should tell you something? I don't want to speak to you.'

'Please Romy. Let me explain. I miss you.'

'Well, I don't miss you!'

'Not even a little bit?' he teased in a voice that used to melt her heart.

'Not even,' she snapped.

'I need to speak to you about the business,' he changed tack smoothly and she had to blink at the speed of the switch.

'What about it?'

'I've had an offer for it,' he added cagily.

'The whole business?'

'Yes. They want both sites.' Romy pulled out a chair and sat down.

'I need to come and talk to you about it, Romy. Please. You own half the Essex centre so it has to be a joint decision.'

'Like the one where you skimmed the profits?'

'I had little choice at the time. I'm sorry. I feel awful about that, so I'm transferring you shares to the same value. If we sell, you'll get your investment and that money back.'

'*If* we sell?' she asked, frowning and making herself stand up to look out across the water to the Bowen boats, which were shining in the sunlight.

'I didn't know if you'd want to come back? The place doesn't run the same without you.'

'Come back?' Romy was incredulous. He wanted her back because the business ran like a dream with her there. Customers liked her and recommended her services to others. What she had discovered since leaving was that, although she loved domestic animals, it was wildlife that held her heart. She liked the untamed survival instincts of the birds she was working with now. Chatting to her tearoom customers all day was hard work, but also fun. That had been the missing ingredient of her old life.

'Without you, the business has lost its soul,' he admitted. 'My heart is still very much with you, too.'

'Oh my God,' she closed her eyes and had to rein in her temper and focus. 'You can't be serious! You're married, Aaron.'

'I need to talk to you about that. Please. I'm coming to London tonight. Let me take you to dinner. We need to talk.'

She put the phone down and then looked up as the door to the tearoom opened. Luca was standing there. Next to him was a bright-eyed little boy who she could tell would be as tall as Luca one day. Both had a shock of dark hair and brown eyes, and they did look like father and son.

'This is Matteo,' said Luca. He had bags under his eyes and he rubbed his neck with his spare hand. 'He's, well. He's my son.' Matteo looked between them with interest and then frowned too, so Romy stepped forward to formally shake his hand, ignoring Luca for a moment because she felt like she might faint at the sight of him and angry little ants were still marching up and down her back from the behaviour of the men in her life. She contained the instinct to bunch her fists and stamp her feet, because Matteo was staring at her.

'Lovely to meet you, Matteo!' she said, keeping her voice friendly and light. Her eyes met Luca's fleetingly and he gave her a pleading stare.

'Welcome to the Wildlife Tearoom,' she said with a smile that she really didn't feel. She drew Matteo outside the tearoom with her and put her fingers to her lips to tell him to keep quiet. She then lifted one of the nesting boxes she'd built and Matteo's eyes went wide. Nestled inside was a mallard duck. It looked up warily, then seemed to realise there was no threat and settled back down to incubate its eggs.

'Wow!' said Matteo in hushed tones. 'Dad said you are a vet and that we might be lucky enough to get some cake here, but I didn't know you had birds! Is this a conservation site?' he asked.

Romy sat back on her heels in shock, because in a way it was. She gave people a chance to be near the water and the creatures that lived there without disturbing them. It also gave her a chance to rehabilitate the wildlife around the tearoom, as well as work with the local swan sanctuary.

She'd sort of become their onsite vet by default, through visiting them so many times. It filled the void created by leaving her own practice. She was using her old skills but in a new way, and it brought balance to her life. She didn't make any money from it, and it took a fair bit of her time, but she couldn't have cared less! She was so much happier, she realised – but then her mood tumbled as she noticed Luca watching her.

'It is, kind of, I guess.' She could feel Luca move to stand behind her, which was good as she couldn't bear to look directly at him. 'I can definitely find some cake for you as well.' She moved to pass Luca, but he caught her arm gently.

'I'm sorry, Romy.'

He looked so troubled that she almost gave in, but instead she slapped on a bright smile for Matteo and brushed past him.

'The boat isn't open today, so I need to finish tidying up,' Romy said, as humour sparked in Luca's eyes and his lips twitched. Romy huffed. The outside of the boat might have been a mess for ages, but the inside was always clean.

She paused as a small hand slipped into hers, and Matteo walked alongside her. She frowned at Luca but he just shrugged and followed them. She led Matteo to a table inside and found him a gooey chocolate cupcake that had a glistening chocolate icing. Matteo breathed in the chocolaty scent of it and then looked at his dad to see if it was ok to eat it. Luca nodded with a smile.

'Not the ideal breakfast, but you are on holiday,' he said, putting a hand on his son's back as he passed, as if feeling he was real and sitting there in front of them.

'Can I go and sit with the ducks to eat this?' Luca looked to Romy.

'Just don't let Bob or any of the others steal your cake. It's not good for their digestion. It might make them sick.'

'Bob?' asked Matteo.

'You'll know him when you see him. He's quite tame and bobs up when you least expect him. He gives me a fright at least twice a day.' Matteo jumped up in excitement and picked up his plate. 'Just stay away from the guard rails and the swans,' she advised and Matteo nodded and rushed off.

They watched him settle at one of her tables nearest the birds and start talking to the ducks.

'Can you ever forgive me?' Luca asked, as soon as Matteo was safely seated outside.

'You brought your son as what? A barrier?'

'He wanted to meet you,' he said simply, moving closer and taking her hand, but she shook him off and glanced at Matteo, who was happily eating his cake and looking at the river.

'He doesn't know me.'

'I've told him about you.'

Romy closed her eyes for a moment and leaned on the sideboard for support. 'When? Today? What did you say?' She wanted to know.

'Weeks ago. When we began spending a lot of time together. I've not introduced him to another woman before, so I wanted to ease the way.'

'But...but...'

'I know. I'm so sorry. I should have told you about him.'

'Why didn't you?' she asked.

'I needed to know he was ok with it first.'

Romy flinched and she wished she'd tried to eat something that morning as her stomach was heaving with the slight movement of the boat when it usually calmed her.

'With what?'

'With me having a girlfriend.'

Romy sank into the nearest chair and he pulled up the closest one, their knees touching. 'He's been through so much change that I'm scared of him pushing me away.'

'Surely you are even closer now? He knows you're his dad no matter what.' She looked at him through hooded eyes and wished her hands didn't itch to slide along his leg and wind around his waist to pull him nearer. Luca rubbed his jaw, which was slightly stubbled that day, and sat back in his chair. 'You look tired,' she said.

His lips quirked with humour and he gazed at her. 'Give it to me straight,' he joked lamely. 'Bianca – my ex-wife – is a nightmare. She has no real interest in me until she feels it can cause the utmost trouble and then she steps in. She's having second-husband issues.'

Romy felt kind of relieved that Bianca had re-married, but it felt weird talking to Luca about her. 'What's that got to do with you?' Then she had an awful thought. 'She wants you back?'

Luca laughed sardonically. 'No. She just enjoys playing with me when she's bored. She dangles meetings with Matteo in front of me and then switches it up. She tried to stay at my place last night, which I refused, but luckily Matteo wanted a sleepover, so she left him with me instead and went to find someone else to torment.'

'I'm not sure I want to get into the middle of all this,' she said, her lip wobbling.

'Please, Romy,' pleaded Luca, kissing her wrist. 'Bianca is another reason I hadn't told you about Matteo yet. I know you don't like married men and I didn't want this exact scenario to happen. I'm single... or I was, until I fell in love with you.'

Romy gasped and covered her mouth with her hand but Matteo chose that moment to wander in with his empty plate and a friendly duck at his feet.

'He likes me!' he cried happily as Bob toddled along beside him.

'He shouldn't really be inside,' she told Matteo, who ushered Bob back out again. She didn't want to meet Luca's gaze, because her heartbeat was pumping at a hundred miles an hour.

'What happened to his tail?' asked Matteo, walking over and pulling out a chair at the table.

'Probably another angry duck, or a fox. Ducks can lose feathers from stress near their tail or rump if they've been attacked. He should moult and grow new ones as it gets nearer to autumn,' she reassured.

'Do you want to come with us to the zoo?' asked Matteo.

Romy didn't know where to look. Luca had just pretty much given his heart to her, but she wasn't ready to forgive him for all his secrets just yet.

'I really should spend the day tidying up. We had a party here yesterday for my grandmother's half-birthday.'

Matteo's eyes lit up and he giggled. 'What's a half-birthday? I've never heard of that before.'

'That's because my grandmother made them up to get her friends and family to bring her extra gifts!' Romy chuckled, rolling her eyes.

'I like the sound of that! Can I meet her?' he asked innocently, and Romy's eyes met Lucas's.

'Umm... not today, but another time.'

'The boat looks pretty clean to me, and you could teach me about the animals at the zoo?' Matteo said as he pressed his fingertips to his plate and then licked the last few cupcake crumbs from them. Both he and Luca looked at her pleadingly and she sighed and stood up, removing her apron and folding it neatly.

'It's years since I've been to London Zoo. You've persuaded me.'

Matteo jumped up and down in glee and Luca looked relieved. He held out his hand to her.

Romy picked up her bag and keys to lock the tearoom and then entwined her fingers with Luca's, hoping she'd made the right decision and that he wouldn't break her heart... again.

Chapter 20

Romy watched people bustling around, craning their necks to see the different animals. An owl display had just begun and the family next to them rushed to grab a place on the tiered seating, almost knocking Romy off her feet. Luca put his arm around her protectively and guided her to a quieter spot while Matteo watched the birds from a few feet away.

'Are you ok?' Luca asked Romy.

'It's just a lot to take in.'

'I don't mean to push you, but it would be good to know how you feel about me.'

'Truthfully, after last night, I'm not sure,' she admitted. 'I understand your reasoning about the secrecy, but still, you did have plenty of opportunity to tell me your situation. Especially when I was so open about what happened with Aaron, and about not being able to have children of my own.'

'I know. I'm sorry.' He hung his head, but then looked at her with beseeching eyes. 'I didn't know how to bring up the fact that I'd married in haste when I was young, and that I regretted everything about it except for my son. Finding out he wasn't biologically mine nearly broke me. It's not an easy thing to come out with.'

'He was the reason you moved here?'

'Yes. When Bianca left, it was a double-edged sword. I was finally free of her demands, but I also lost my son. Not only had Matteo's biological father taken my wife, he took my son, too.'

'She was the one who cheated on you?'

'Yes. We dated from *scuola superiore* – high school. She was dazzling to me. She was confident and popular and I got swept along for the ride. The problem was that she craved attention constantly and didn't mind who she got it from. She bores easily, and by the time she was twenty-one she was pregnant. We married and that was that.'

'You didn't think she might have cheated?'

'Yes, I did, but I felt I couldn't ask her if I was the father. It might have destroyed her. I did ask questions later, but she's a good actress and we argued.' He shook his head in disbelief at his own stupidity, it seemed. 'I felt ashamed to have asked her. We did the best we could to recover, but it was never quite the same. I felt I couldn't trust her and I was right. When Matteo was four, Guiseppe turned up demanding to see his son.'

'Oh Luca, I'm so sorry.'

Romy took his hand in hers but his eyes were glazed as he looked down at it. She tried to imagine if someone had told Arthur's girlfriend Daisy that her daughter Brontë wasn't hers, and how she'd react. It would crush her. Romy didn't think Daisy would ever recover. Brontë was her world. Now Romy's brother was getting broody and would do anything to protect Brontë, who wasn't his biological child. Relationships could be messy, she realised.

'I just didn't know how to tell you,' Luca went on. 'You were heartbreakingly honest about your situation, but I don't need more children. Matteo is my son, no matter what, but he's enough. I don't need a brood of mini-Lucases running around. I'm exhausted running my business with one child I don't see often enough.'

Romy froze at the mention of a future, because this was all going too fast for her. Was Luca trying to tell her that it didn't matter if she couldn't conceive? That he loved her anyway?

'I'm meeting Aaron tonight,' she blurted out and Luca shrank back in his chair.

'Because I messed up?' he asked angrily, then glanced over to check on Matteo, who was playing happily with some other kids next to the falconry display.

'No. Because he wants to talk to me about the business I left.'

'He wants you back?' his fists bunched and his eyes blazed.

'Possibly, but I don't want him. I will never want him,' she said furiously. The problem was that although Luca wanted to believe her, a tiny seed of doubt had already begun to grow, and its roots were dragging him down with them. She could tell by the sudden mistrust on his face. 'Luca,' she reiterated. 'Aaron is in my past.'

'That's what Bianca said about Guiseppe,' he muttered under his breath.

Romy frowned, as she hadn't quite caught what he said, but then Matteo called them over, so she shrugged and went with Luca to see what he wanted.

'Can you tell me all about the owls?' Matteo asked, excitement in his voice, his body bobbing up and down as he went up on tiptoes to squint over the rows of people. Luca swung him up onto his shoulders, so that Matteo could see better for a few minutes, before swinging him back to the floor.

'This one is a spectacled owl,' said Romy, pointing to the bird the handler was carefully holding. 'They come from Central or South America and live in rainforests or open woodland. They have a ring of paler feathers around their eyes that give them their name,' she grinned, pointing the unique facial features out. Matteo seemed fascinated and grabbed her hand as they walked along, which made Luca and Romy exchange glances. He reached for Luca's hand too and they wandered around happily for the next few hours, eating strawberry ice cream and feeding the elephants from their hands at feeding time, which made Matteo giggle in delight.

Her back was aching from a restless night, but she was happy, Romy decided. She still needed to unpack all her emotions over Luca's past, but now she felt a glimmer of hope that they could work it out. She just needed to steer clear of Bianca.

Chapter 21

'Are you sure you want to do this?' Clara fussed around her and handed her a soft blue summer jumper to put on if she got cold later. There had been a slight breeze coming off the river when she'd checked on the birds earlier.

There hadn't been a break-in for a while and Romy felt sure her new CCTV would prevent further trouble. A hedge separated the dock from the path, and the security lighting Arthur had installed was bound to put potential troublemakers off. The boat next door being occupied helped. Greg, who had moved in recently, often waved to her and said hello when she opened up the tearoom, or closed for the night.

Aaron was standing outside her boat as she approached, a wide smile forming at the sight of her. She knew she looked good. Maybe not as polished as he'd remember, but she did brush her hair more often now, so that she didn't scare her customers away. She'd even bought herself a couple of pairs of new jeans. Her short-sleeved blouse was the colour of a summer sky and complimented her skin tone. Tonight she had left her hair to flow around her shoulders, because she knew how much Aaron loved it when she swept it up into a high ponytail as it gave him a chance to kiss her neck. He was wearing smart deep blue trousers and a crisp long-sleeved white shirt. His short blond hair had been stylishly cut and he was clean-shaven. She waited for the arrow to her heart at the sight of the handsome man she'd loved for so long, but she just felt disgust.

Aaron's smile suggested he expected her to welcome him, but she scowled and walked up to meet him, standing just far enough apart that he couldn't touch her or kiss her in greeting. 'It's good to see you,' he said, leaning forward and kissing her cheek anyway. Romy cringed and stepped back, just in time to see Luca watching them from across the water, a scowl on his face. She gulped and refused to be intimidated by either of them.

'Where are we going? I'm starving.' Romy had never admitted to Aaron when she was hungry before, because he always gave her a disapproving look. He expected his girlfriend to stay trim and eat healthily, like he did. Joy was sucked out of eating anything frivolous, so this time Romy was determined to scoff a huge meal in front of him and get him to pay. Aaron raised an eyebrow but said nothing. 'I hope you're not taking me to a fancy place where they serve a morsel of food and call it haute cuisine?' she asked as she started walking to his sleek bottle-green sports car which she was sure he loved more than anyone. He was always washing it and wiping specks of mud from the wheels.

'There is a new fish restaurant just up the river,' he suggested, naming a fancy place with bottles of wine costing more than she made in a week.

'Aaron. I know we only lived together for four years, but you should remember I'm a vegetarian,' she seethed.

'I thought you might have got over that by now?' He chuckled at his own joke and her mood soured further.

She'd only agreed to a meal because she knew she'd probably throw something at him if they weren't somewhere public. Ignoring him, she directed him to her favourite restaurant. They had a huge vegetarian section to their menu, and she could get drunk. Alcohol turned her stomach, lately, but she was determined to have a glass of expensive wine. In fact, she'd been off a lot of things that she usually ate, or drank. She suddenly frowned, counting back, and realising she hadn't had a period for ages. They had always been terribly irregular, so she hadn't thought much about it, but now she realised it had been months since the last one. She knew that stress often disrupted her already messy cycle, so Luca and Aaron were both equally to blame.

'I booked a table at the other place,' Aaron complained when they arrived, but was silenced by her look. 'This seems delightful,' he added, not disguising his sarcasm.

The restaurant was more of a pub, with smoke grey frontage, huge bay windows to the river and a beautifully planted terrace with round tables and chairs dotted all around, separated by big planters of miniature trees and trailing ivy. Fairy lights twinkled across the courtyard as the sky grew darker and Romy's tummy rumbled in anticipation of some food that she might keep down. She hadn't been feeling one hundred percent for a while now and Aaron turning up wasn't helping. Her body felt tense and she kept looking over her shoulder in case Luca popped up. She pictured his angry face when she'd told him about this meeting and she could kind of understand why, but it really was nothing to do with him. He had enough going on with Matteo and Bianca – his secret son and wife. It was a theme in her life, it seemed, and she was sick of it.

They were led to a quiet table next to the windows overlooking the river. To an innocent onlooker, they possibly looked like a couple, but Romy couldn't wait to leave, even though they'd only just arrived!

She quickly scanned the menu and ordered pea and broad bean gnocchi with brown sugar and basil pesto, and some garlic bread. Aaron hated it when she ate garlic bread, so she would enjoy every bite, even if she threw it up later. Just as the waiter was about to leave, she caught his arm and added an avocado, feta, chilli and lime salad as well. Disapproval sparked in Aaron's eyes as he watched her.

'Hungry?'

'Ravenous.'

'Do you come here often?'

'Not as often as I'd like,' she said. 'I'm working my guts out to repay the loan I borrowed from my sister to set my new business up, because my old partner stole from me,' she added sweetly and he flinched.

'I really am sorry, Romy.' He tried to take her hand across the table but she moved it out of reach. 'Will you let me explain?'

'Go ahead.' She did actually want to hear this. He'd given loads of excuses since they had parted but none had rung true. 'The truth, if you're capable.' He winced and ordered a bottle of Merlot, but she shook her head at the waiter because she'd just decided she needed to be sober for this and asked for water instead.

'Gemma is a demanding wife.' He pulled a face when anger showed in Romy's expression. 'We really were about to separate when you and I got together, but then I found out she was pregnant again.' His eyes pleaded with her for understanding but her jaw dropped and she felt like she might be sick.

'Your wife... who you were still married to and clearly sleeping with... was pregnant?' she clarified, the breath hissing out of her, so she held onto the edge of the table for support.

'With twins,' he rushed out, as if he needed to say it quickly. 'It's why I had to travel back to Wales so often to check on the other practice and see the children. Gemma was used to me working away a lot and so were you, but it was all very stressful for me...' Romy went to stand up but he caught her hand. 'I need to explain.' She stayed sitting, but her legs were braced to leave and her eyes and mind were full of fire, her skin flushing with anger. 'Gemma always wants the best of everything. The best house, car and designer labels. We have a live-in nanny, for goodness sake! It was too much. When I met you, you weren't interested in any of that. I've never met anyone who cared less.'

'So, you thought you'd take advantage of me?'

'No. It was a breath of fresh air. I fell in love with you.'

Romy scoffed in disgust. Luca had used that line – after he told her he'd lied to her too. 'You've only ever loved yourself,' she shot back.

'I've officially separated from Gemma and want you back – in the vet practice, as well as in my bed.'

'You can't be serious.'

'I've missed you.'

'It's been over two years.'

'It took a while to get Gemma to agree to a divorce.'

'You told me you were already divorced!'

He hung his head. 'I know. I didn't mean to lie, but she wouldn't let me go.'

'You didn't want to go, you mean. You just kept seeing both of us. You're just as high maintenance as you say she is, with your sports car and our fancy flat.'

'She seduced me that first Christmas, when I told her I was leaving... for you.' The colour drained out of Romy's face.

'Your wife knew about me?'

'Yes. She got pregnant to make me stay.'

'Your own wife seduced you? Oh my God, you are a moron. You then spent four years seeing us both? Splitting your time between two families and parts of the country?'

Aaron's skin flushed and he wouldn't meet her eyes suddenly. 'Well yes... I didn't have much choice. Gemma knew I'd be a way a lot with the second site. She'd agreed to it. I couldn't lose you, but my children needed me. It was all getting too expensive though, so I borrowed from our business. I'm sorry.'

'Borrowed?' she almost spat out. 'Were you happy I couldn't have children?' she asked, and the world stopped moving when he paused to look at his hands and then slowly gave his answer.

'Gemma had lovers early on in our marriage but I forgave her. We kind of had an open marriage, until I fell in love with you and wanted to leave her. Gemma and I both agreed no children with anyone else, for the sake of our children.'

'So... what does that mean?' Romy felt the blood drain from her body, as she feared what was coming next.

'I had a vasectomy after the twins were born,' he admitted sheepishly. She sprung to her feet at this, and her chair fell to the floor with a clunk, startling a sheepdog that was slumbering under the next table.

Romy apologised to his owner and stood over Aaron without touching him. 'Romy, sit down,' he pleaded. 'I love you. I didn't mean to hurt you.'

'You let me go to countless medical appointments, cry

into my pillow and crave a child of my own for years before realising it wasn't going to happen for me. You comforted me.' She was shouting now and a few heads turned their way. 'You let me think I couldn't have children, when all the time you'd had a vasectomy!' she said incredulously, her fists bunching because she was certainly going to hit him.

Before she could, Arthur and Daisy rushed over from the other side of the restaurant, where they had been having a rare date night. Arthur pulled Romy into his side, his demeanour telling Aaron not to get up. It was clear they'd heard the last sentence of their conversation – as had half the pub, presumably – but Romy was beyond caring. Tears were streaming down her face unchecked as Daisy led her away.

'Do not contact my sister again, ever,' growled Arthur, as he leant close to Aaron's face. Aaron gulped and nodded. 'You'll be hearing from my solicitor about the sale of the practice. You're lucky Romy doesn't want to call the police about your theft from the business. You had seriously better get out of town before you find out just how angry I am.'

Aaron sidled out of his seat and took one last longing look at Romy, who was by now huddled at Daisy's table, her shoulders bobbing as she sobbed. Then he quickly grabbed his jacket and vacated the building.

Chapter 22

Luca woke with a start and realised he must have fallen asleep last night with the television on. He picked his phone up from where it had fallen on the floor and checked the time. It was still early, so he groaned and heaved himself into a sitting position. Knowing Romy had been with Aaron the previous evening had stirred something inside him. He hadn't liked it, and he'd come home and waited for her text.

When it hadn't arrived, the self-doubt and worry had seeped in and he'd poured himself a hefty glass of Pinot Noir, and then a second and third. Now his head was pounding. Looking around at the mess of his usually pristine flat he sighed, throwing two headache tablets into his mouth dry and wincing at the bitter taste. His clothes were strewn on the floor and the takeaway he'd ordered was still in the bag on his coffee table, making the room smell foul.

Getting up and throwing the dinner straight in the bin, Luca bent to pick up his clothes and fold them over the back of his grey-blue velvet couch. He'd always loved the clean lines and uncluttered space, but since living with Romy at the bungalow, he could see it was a bit clinical and unloved. He did have a tiny curated selection of family photos in silver frames on his sleek black sideboard now, but other than that, his personality didn't shine through anywhere.

He pictured the tea boat with its rows and rows of artisan coffee mugs made by a local potter, and the beautiful river scenes with birds that Maya had painted for her sister as a gift when she'd rebranded as the Wildlife Tearoom. The whole place shone with Romy's personality. Before the tidy-up, he'd been drawn to spend time with her, even if it was just to wind her up to make her notice him. Why hadn't she called him last night after her meal with Aaron? His stomach sank at the thought that she might want her old life back, if Aaron had sold it well enough. Luca wanted to believe it was over with her and her ex, but the fact that he'd seen multiple texts pop up on the home screen of her phone while they'd been living together did make Luca wonder if there was still something there.

Bianca was still playing up and trying to join him and Matteo wherever they went. Her games were exhausting. His phone trilled. He looked at the caller ID and groaned.

'Bianca,' he sighed restlessly. 'What can I do for you?'

'You sound grouchy, *amore mio*,' she purred.

'I'm not your love,' he pointed out automatically.

'Of course you are. You're my first love,' she laughed.

He rolled his eyes. 'Bianca. I'm busy.'

'Can you see us today?'

'I am going to be at work, but I will always find time for my son.'

'See,' she pointed out. 'Grouchy!'

'What time are you thinking of?' He picked up the plate and cutlery he'd laid out for his untouched dinner and shoved them back in the kitchen cupboard and drawer.

They made a satisfying clunk and he was surprised the plate didn't break in half. It would have suited his current mood.

'I'm feeling bored, as Giuseppe is always working. Matteo is fed up too.'

'Why don't you take him somewhere nice for the day?' Luca suggested through gritted teeth.

'I thought it would be more fun with you,' she flirted.

He seethed. She knew he was self-employed and was out on the boats most days, yet she thought it was ok to flit in and out of his life and disrupt him whenever she had nothing better to do. It showed how little she respected him, or even knew him, these days. If she thought he'd ever go back to her after the way she'd treated him, then she was more of a fool than he was.

Luca was trying to focus on his son and keep up with the growing pressure from his brother to expand the business. He had never been successful enough for Bianca in Italy. A friend had employed Luca to assist in running his printing firm, as he was trained in business management and marketing. It had helped massively when the brothers had decided to relocate to the U.K. and had taken over the boats. Alex and Luca had grown up around the water so being on the river was second nature to them. They'd visited their *nonno* regularly as children and been taught to assist with the cruises during their holidays.

Now that he was successful, with a fleet of cruise liners and a fancy penthouse flat, Bianca suddenly wanted more from him. She craved his attention and his energy, and wanted to interfere with his time with his child. Her husband was a millionaire too, and far richer than Luca, so why the hell she kept trying to mess with him, he didn't know – but he'd had enough.

'I'll pick Matteo up after work,' he said tersely. Then he sat up and rubbed his stubbly chin, wincing at the thought of having to spend one more moment with Bianca, and then groaning in frustration. Maybe there was trouble in paradise? The thought that her marriage might be on the rocks terrified him!

Chapter 23

Maya scooted down to sit next to her sister, who was on the floor, her back to a radiator that wasn't on, her arms wrapped around her knees as she rested her head on them. Romy lifted her head briefly to look at Maya, but didn't have the energy to raise it again.

'Arthur called me,' said Maya. She tenderly brushed Romy's hair out of her eyes and kissed the top of her head. Then she rested her head against Romy's for a moment and hugged her shoulders. Romy sobbed and sank into the hug, wrapping her arms around her sister as she cried.

'What happened?' Maya asked. 'Arthur was evasive. He just said you were upset, and that Aaron had been here.'

Romy lifted up her head and rubbed her bloodshot eyes. 'Aaron took me out to dinner to discuss selling the business last night.'

'Ok...' Maya said slowly.

'I wanted to pay back your loan.'

You don't need to do that!'

'I know, but I hate being indebted, even to you.'

'Romy. I'm your big sister,' said Maya gently. 'You are never indebted to me. How can I repay you for all of the hours of support you gave me setting up my jewellery business, or all the times you let me sit on your boat drinking tea and drawing the river. We could call it rent!'

Romy gave her sister a lopsided watery smile and then sniffed. Maya handed her some tissues which she took gratefully as they both stood up.

'I'm going to make us both some hot sweet tea,' Maya said, leading Romy into the little kitchen at the back of the property with its window looking over the vast back garden. The kitchen was one of Romy's favourite places, because it was warm and inviting, with its ceramic pots overflowing with trailing plants on practically every counter. Clara always filled her fridge with tempting morsels of food, too. Then she remembered Luca cooking her meals here, including the one that he'd brought up to the dock, and her lip wobbled.

'Where's Clara?' asked Maya as she handed Romy a steaming mug of tea.

Romy blew on the cup and then sipped gratefully. 'She's gone for a walk along the river. She does that most mornings.'

The sugar settled in her stomach, as there hadn't been much else there lately. She hadn't eaten the meal she'd been looking forward to at the pub the previous evening, and then had immediately gone to bed when she got back, assuring Arthur and Daisy that she was fine.

'Have you eaten?' Maya pulled a couple of croissants from her bag. She must have grabbed them from the Riverside café across the water. They were big and crumbly and Romy took one and pulled it apart, but didn't eat any. Maya gave her a hard stare, so she nibbled on a piece of flaky pastry while Maya buttered the rest and added some tangy apricot jam.

'What happened?' Maya nudged Romy's plate forward and urged her to eat, so she did take a few bites. It felt good to have some sustenance.

Romy sighed and sipped her tea again before beginning. She couldn't quite believe what Aaron had told her. She'd spent the night tossing and turning, after realising how selfishly he'd behaved and how his lies had altered the course of her life. Her body had been wracked with sob after sob until she had nothing left to give.

'He told me that his wife got pregnant just after he met me... with twins.'

Maya's eyebrows shot into her hairline and she grabbed the edge of the counter to steady herself, but she stayed silent. Romy could see she was grinding her teeth by the set of her jaw.

'He was trying to leave her for me, apparently, and she 'persuaded' him to have sex before he left,' Romy continued.

Maya's eyes were almost out on stalks now and Romy could imagine steam coming out of her ears.

'So, he told her about you and she didn't want him to leave?' Maya asked.

Romy nodded. 'When they found out she was pregnant he couldn't go. He split his time between us. I was busy running the second practice and felt proud that he was a multiple business owner. We had discussed him selling the centre in Wales and buying another site closer to Essex, so he would be at home more.'

The word home, made Romy's stomach heave. It had all been a lie. 'He was clearly never going to do that either.

Then once she'd had the twins, they decided there would be no more children.'

'He shouldn't have begun his relationship with you until he was single,' said Maya angrily. 'Or he should have told you he was still married and you could have made your own decision.' Then she frowned and moved her mug and plate out of the way to rest her arms on the little breakfast bar. 'Hang on... he didn't want more children? But you tried for years... That doesn't make sense. Maybe he just didn't want more children with her?' Maya clarified.

Romy felt bile fill her throat. 'No,' she sighed, closing her eyes as pain sliced through her back and stomach and she groaned and rubbed her tummy. Her stomach had been sore all night and she shifted uncomfortably. 'He had a vasectomy soon after,' she explained, rubbing eyes that were already sore from hours of crying. Saying it out loud was like another knife to her heart. 'He didn't want to finance any more children.'

The colour drained out of Maya's face and she gasped and covered her mouth with her hand, tears springing to her eyes. She got up and flew into her sister's arms where they both cried silently for what felt like hours.

'Oh Romy. I'm so sorry.' Maya wiped tears from her face. 'What an absolute bastard. How dare he ever have said he loved you, when he treated you that way. I'll kill him!'

Romy gave her sister a watery smile and Maya started opening cupboards in search of wine. Romy refused a glass and Maya frowned again and then raised her eyebrows.

Romy looked uncomfortable. 'I slept with Luca without protection because I'm stupid. I was in the throes of lust and thought I couldn't get pregnant...' her bottom lip wobbled and Maya's eyes went wide. She looked at Romy's hands protectively cradling her slightly swollen stomach and then back at her sister. 'We've used birth control ever since. I even stored some in my make-up bag next to the shower because I can't seem to control myself when his body is all sexy and wet.'

'Oh my God! Too much information!' Maya put her hands over her ears for a moment and then dropped them as Romy's words sunk in. 'Romy!'

'I'm not sure, but I've been feeling sick for weeks, and now I'm getting a shooting pain around my back.'

'Bloody hell, Romy,' said Maya as she started looking around in a panic and then grabbed her handbag and searched for her phone, immediately dialling their doctor's surgery and asking for an emergency appointment. Romy tried to protest, but in the end, she was just too tired to argue, and she did have a niggling worry that there might be a baby growing in her tummy. She already felt fiercely protective over it, even though she had no clue if it was even possible.

'I might just have a bug,' she shrugged as Maya eased a jumper around her shoulders as if she was fragile porcelain and ushered her out to her car.

Clara came in and gave Maya a worried stare. 'Everything ok?'

'Um... yes. Romy has a stomach bug, so I'm taking her to the doctor,' Maya smiled a bit manically. Romy tried not to laugh. Her sister was usually calm personified, but right now she looked like she'd just run through a bush. Her hair was all over the place where she'd run her hands through it while waiting for someone at the surgery to answer her call.

'Let me know if you need anything,' said Clara with a worried frown.

'We will,' Romy replied as Maya rushed her into her car and slammed the door in her face.

Chapter 24

Romy could get used to being pampered. She was still in bed at 10am and the little side table next to her bed was cluttered with power drinks, chocolates and a fresh cup of tea that Clara had just brought her.

Maya had arrived with a bag of goodies earlier that morning and insisted Romy take a day off while she ran the tea boat with Clara for the day. Neither of them had a clue what they were doing, but they'd muddle through, they'd assured her.

There was no swaying her sister once she'd made a decision, so Romy wriggled her toes and grabbed one of the romance reads that her grandmother had sent round. She'd chickened out of telling any of them the news that the doctor had told her, except for Maya. They all thought she had a tummy bug, but she had an idea that Clara might have seen the pregnancy vitamins Maya had insisted she start to take before she'd slid the packet into her drawer that morning. Clara hadn't asked any questions, but she had looked troubled, which Romy would have worried about, if she hadn't been ecstatically happy to be told she was pregnant. After peeing on a test stick and having a few other tests over the past few days, she'd been assured she was fine and was now booked in for a scan.

'You must limit your stress,' the kind doctor had scolded her, and Maya had nodded almost manically and then told her she was not to turn up for work for at least a few days and that they could manage all week if she needed them. Romy was already itching to get back to her boat and her birds, but she knew she needed to get her head around her new predicament first. She wondered if she'd got pregnant during the first night of unexpected passion with Luca. They'd used protection after that moment of madness that had linked them together forever. She wanted to get used to the idea herself first before she told anyone else, and had sworn her sister to secrecy.

'Surely you want to tell Luca?' Maya had been surprised.

'Of course,' Romy had replied. 'But I need to get my head round it myself first. I'm still reeling from all the lies Aaron told me. I might have got pregnant years ago if he'd told the truth and I'd met someone else. You know I always dreamt of being a young mum. He stole that from me.'

Romy hugged her knees to her stomach and didn't know how to process the shock of what Aaron had done.

'You aren't exactly ancient,' Maya laughed and Romy chuckled too, because her sister was right.

'So many unnecessary doctors' appointments, though,' she'd mumbled tearfully to Maya. It was difficult to get hold of her emotions after all the deceit. She wondered if that was how Luca felt about Bianca, and her heart broke a little for him too.

Romy had to stay calm for the sake of her baby. The

doctor hadn't been unduly worried about her stomach pains, and said it was probably her muscles stretching to accommodate the still-tiny foetus, but she was glad they were going to do a scan anyway. Her mind was a hot mess of emotions. She still couldn't quite believe that a baby was growing in her tummy and she was going to be responsible for its happiness. What if she was a useless mother and fouled it all up?

There was a light knock on the door, and Luca peeped his head round it. Her heart swelled at the sight of him, but she also quickly covered herself up again with the duvet and was tongue-tied, which was unusual for her. Her face warmed as he came and sat on her side of the bed and gently brushed her hair out of her eyes.

'Shouldn't you be at work?' she asked, for something to say.

'I was worried about you. *Nonna* said you're unwell. There are queues of dog walkers at your tea boat,' he said with a chuckle, then put a hand out to calm her when she tried to get out of bed. 'Your sister is handling everything well. *Nonna* has everyone lined up like soldiers waiting their turn and no one is complaining. They asked after you when I popped by.'

He held up a bag of cupcakes for her and placed two takeaway coffees on the chest of drawers.

'Thanks,' she said coolly, not really knowing how to respond. They'd had a great day with Matteo at the zoo, but all she could think of now was Aaron's revelations, and the fact that she'd let someone treat her that way. Luca had kept secrets from her too. Now she had one of her own, and she wasn't ready to share it yet.

Matteo was going to have a brother or sister and Bianca would be part of Romy's life. She wasn't sure she wanted to live looking over her shoulder to see if the ex-wife had won Luca back, or hatched another dastardly plan to ruin their lives. She'd be in the same situation if she took Aaron back, and that life was not for her. She had her baby to think about now and until she'd had the first scan and checked everything was ok, there wasn't much point in telling him, she reasoned. Supposing the doctor had made a mistake and she'd just had a tummy bug? Maybe it had been a faulty pregnancy test... He'd probably run away at the first sign of trouble anyway.

He leaned in to kiss her, but she recoiled and he seemed taken aback. 'I'm sorry. I thought...' he frowned and sat back. He was wearing a fitted black Bowen Brothers short-sleeved shirt that she loved, with smart black jeans. His jet-black hair was slightly shorter than yesterday, so he must have had a haircut that morning. Who was he trying to impress? Her – or Bianca? She hated feeling vulnerable like this. He looked around the room uncomfortably. 'Are you still angry with me?' he asked.

'Not really,' she admitted, 'but I think I need some space. Your son is here and he needs you, so perhaps that will give me a bit of time to decide what I want... what I need.'

He took her hand and kissed the back of her wrist, making sparks jump on her skin. 'I love you,' he said sadly and she knew he wanted to hear her say the words back. 'Have I ruined this?'

'I don't know,' she said honestly and her eyes filled with tears. Blinking them away, she brushed her hand across her cheeks, but he cupped her face in his hands and kissed her ever so sweetly on the lips before standing up and brushing down his jeans. She wanted him to take her in his arms and tell her that everything was going to be ok, but the look he gave her told her she was breaking his heart and he straightened his shoulders and stood tall.

'I should probably get back to work.'

'Ok,' she answered, not meaning it. She went to get up but he stopped her.

'I can see myself out.' He turned and left the room, but as he reached the door a delivery woman was walking up the front path with a bouquet of deep red roses so huge that it blocked out her head and filled the air with the scent of heady musk. The woman turned and smiled brightly at Luca. 'Well, one lucky lady lives here!'

'I can take them for her,' said Luca with a false smile. He thanked her and retraced his steps to place the flowers on the breakfast bar for Romy, trying not to notice the scrolled handwritten card from Aaron saying how much she meant to him, that he was sorry and he loved her.

Chapter 25

'Can we visit Romy?' asked Matteo as he ran ahead of his dad down the dock towards their boats. All of this would belong to Matteo and his cousins one day – if his brother Alex ever managed to date someone for more than a week.

'Not right now,' he called after his son, his heart sinking at having to explain to Matteo that she didn't want to see his father, but would probably welcome a visit from his son. Matteo and Bianca were travelling home later that day, so he did really want Romy to see Matteo before he left.

'But she loved visiting the zoo with us,' said his son innocently. Luca smiled at that. The day had been filled with laughter and ice cream. The sun had blazed down and Romy had insisted that they all buy matching animal-themed baseball caps to shield their eyes. He pulled out his phone and looked at the photo, their three smiling faces staring at him, and he decided he needed to get a backbone. Losing Romy was not an option, so he would let her have her space... but within reason. He needed to reassure her about how much she meant to him.

'Luca!' called Bianca from behind him and he cringed. She was walking arm in arm with Alex, who looked about as happy as someone on their way to the dentist for an extraction. Bianca loved flirting with Alex in front of him and Luca knew Alex only put up with her for Matteo's sake. They all had to play nice.

'Bianca,' he replied, his voice tight. 'I thought you were leaving Matteo with me today so he can help me on the cruises? He's looking forward to it.'

'I thought I'd join him,' she gave a tinkly little laugh that grated on his nerves.

'Bored again...' said Alex into his ear as he passed and managed to untangle himself from his ex-sister-in-law. Bianca was dressed for the sun in a deep red flowing summer dress and high heels, which made her look like she was going to visit the racecourse down river. She had dark sunglasses perched on her nose and a designer handbag over her shoulder.

'Are we taking you to the races?' asked Alex, with a hopeful tone as he ruffled his nephew's hair and they grinned at each other.

'No. I'll stay for the first return cruise and then maybe you can buy Matteo and me lunch?' she pushed her sunglasses onto her head as her dark hair flowed around her shoulders. She'd always been beautiful, but she was even prettier as she aged. Luca closed his eyes for a moment to calm his temper and then looked at his son, who was practically hopping from foot to foot in excitement. Guiseppe worked in a bank and never invited Matteo to his offices, where he would 'get under his feet'. Luca rolled his eyes at the memory of hearing him say that at one of their infrequent meetings. He was about to try and get out of the lunch, but Bianca interrupted. 'We are going home tomorrow, of course, so I could take him last minute shopping instead?'

Luca seethed inside, as her subtle blackmailing was exhausting. He was already juggling work, Romy and Matteo, thanks to this unexpected visit, and now Bianca was playing up too. 'Let's see how busy we get,' he sighed as he walked away to catch up with Matteo and left Bianca to trail along behind them.

The boat slid expertly into the dock a while later with Alex at its helm and Luca glanced at his watch, surprised to see it was already after midday. He sighed and rubbed his back where he'd been tossing and turning all night. Romy wanting space was a niggling worry and Bianca chatting up all his male guests on the cruise back irritated the hell out of him. The woman was relentless.

'She thinks it will make you jealous,' noted Alex as he saw what his brother was looking at. Bianca was sunning herself on deck and pretending not to notice the admiring glances coming her way now.

'She was practically sitting on a guy's lap earlier!' Luca raged.

'Are you?' asked Alex.

'Am I what?'

'Jealous?' They both looked at Bianca as she slid her sunglasses onto her dark silky hair and began chatting to the guy who had just sat next to her, lightly touching his arm and throwing back her head with laughter at whatever he'd just whispered into her ear.

'Never again,' hissed Luca, as he checked that Matteo was happily standing at one of the windows and watching the river out of the window. Luca had spent the past few hours walking him proudly around the boat and introducing his son to new crew. Most of his staff had been with them for a while and already knew Matteo, but Luca never got tired of telling people about his beautiful boy. Alex laughed and slapped him on the back and Luca finally grinned too.

'Take them to lunch. That way we might get rid of her for the afternoon if she gets bored. I can cope here.'

'Are you saying I'm boring?' Luca playfully punched him on the arm, but Alex ducked away, a huge grin on his face.

'If the cap fits, *fratello*,' he chuckled and Luca rolled his eyes, then grinned too as Matteo came over. Luca put his arm around his son's shoulders and hugged him to his side. He would never tire of feeling his son next to him and his heart ached for the inevitable pain of parting again later on.

'Hungry?'

Matteo's eyes lit up, as it seemed he was always ready to eat. He'd grown in height since Luca had last seen him and it burnt his soul not to be with him every day.

'Of course,' his son shouted and hopped from foot to foot in excitement.

'Burgers?'

'Can we?'

'Of course!' Luca parroted and then his mood soured as Bianca joined them. She swished her hair over her shoulder and then glanced behind her to see if her new suitor was still watching.

'I'm taking Matteo to the pub by the river for lunch if you want to join us,' he asked courteously. Bianca pouted.

'I was hoping for something a bit more glamorous.'

'Then go to lunch with Guiseppe,' sniped Luca and then wished he hadn't. His mood always blackened when Bianca was around and he hated himself for that. Alex stepped away and left them to it. Bianca sighed theatrically and then hooked her Chanel handbag further up her shoulder. 'Burgers it is,' she said as she walked towards the starboard side of the boat to disembark.

Luca spoke to a few regular guests as they stepped off the boat, and Bianca seemed to seethe at the number of women who stopped him for a quick chat or question about the boat. He was pleased she knew he was still attractive to others, even though she'd discarded him. He'd tried to give her everything, but it hadn't been enough. He wasn't rich or glamorous enough for her. Now he wondered what he'd ever seen in her and Romy came to mind.

Romy had an unassuming air about her, and didn't judge anyone. She had a fiery temperament and beautiful dark brown eyes, and he quite enjoyed their verbal sparring. Especially if it meant they ended up in bed. Romy wouldn't care where they ate and as he walked into the gastro pub where he'd booked a table, he pictured the times he'd been there with Romy. They had a vegetarian menu she liked. He looked around the grey and green interior of the pub, with lots of lush green plants and velvet seating, and realised she was pretty much all he could think about these days. It was worrying. Letting another person close to his heart was a risk, but he'd already blurted out that he loved her. Not only that, but it was true.

He could see Bianca taking in their surroundings and not being happy about them, but she caught his eye and said nothing. He wondered if she could tell that he wouldn't put up with her troublemaking anymore. He might not be Matteo's biological father, but he felt like it, and Matteo would continue to be his son for the rest of his life. Luca was the one who had stayed up all night with him when he'd had colic as a baby, while Bianca was out partying. Luca had taken Matteo to his doctor's appointments, and shown him love when Bianca hadn't been interested. As he'd grown, she'd come to love him, but she always put herself first, which frustrated the hell out of Luca.

They were led to a booth by the window. Matteo's joy at them all being together was contagious because the adults put their differences aside, and they actually managed not to kill each other while they ordered plump beef burgers, crisp salads and fries. They had just finished their food when Luca looked up to see Romy pass their table. She clearly hadn't been expecting to see them either, as she jumped when Matteo called her name. She smiled nervously when she saw the family eating together, and she looked like she wanted to run, but politeness ruled and she turned and reluctantly walked their way.

'Matteo!' she said happily as he jumped up to hug her. 'Lovely to see you.' Romy glanced nervously at Luca as her arms wrapped around his son. Bianca glared at him simultaneously, straightening her back and tapping her perfectly painted red nails on the table top. Luca was too pleased to see Romy to care much about Bianca, but this first meeting was important.

'We've been on the boats all morning and Dad just bought us burgers,' Matteo told her in excitement. 'I asked Dad if we could see you again, but he said you might be busy.'

Romy gulped and Luca winced, because he knew Matteo would likely have mentioned the lady from the zoo to his mum, but he wasn't sure if he'd mentioned any details.

'Again?' asked Bianca, her voice ice cold as she regarded Romy, who was dressed in a flowy skirt that showed off her beautiful tanned legs, and an oversized T-shirt that hid the rest of her frame.

'Bianca,' said Luca. 'This is Romy.'

'Romy?' she questioned, not smiling at Romy, which made her frown.

'My girlfriend,' he said firmly and Romy's face went bright red!

'Girlfriend? It seems you've already met my son,' Bianca added as she stood up and brushed her dress down unnecessarily before shaking Romy's hand. She looked Romy up and down, but Romy stood firm and refused to fidget, which made his heart melt a little.

'We went to the zoo together,' butted in Matteo. 'I told you.'

'So you did,' mused Bianca. 'I thought it was just one of dad's usual casual dates,' she added scathingly.

Luca paused and tried not to react because he had dated a lot of women, but none had ever met his son, and Bianca knew this full well.

'It seems I'm the last to know about this little scenario,' Bianca continued. She frowned at Romy for a moment and then gave her a mega-watt smile, which Luca knew wasn't genuine. 'Please join us,' she sat down and made room for Romy, but Romy backed away.

'It's great to see you, Matteo, and to meet you, Bianca, but I need to get back to work. I just popped over to help the owner out because a swan has wandered up from the river and ended up in the pub garden.'

'Romy is a vet,' said Matteo proudly. Romy beamed at him and said her goodbyes, but Luca caught up with her by the alcove next to a private dining area.

'I've missed you,' he said heatedly.

'You saw me yesterday!'

'I want to see more of you.' He caught her hips and pulled their bodies close together and his mind filled with mush. His head bent to hers and captured her lips and she couldn't help but wind her hands into his hair and pull him nearer, it seemed, which made him growl and ease her even closer still.

'Luca! Bianca and Matteo are here,' she said breathlessly as they moved apart. 'You said you'd give me space, but you just told your son and ex-wife that I'm your girlfriend before you asked me,' she said crossly, her eyes sparking with anger, her arms crossing protectively across her chest.

'I told you I'd mentioned you to Matteo. Plus we agreed to become official at your grandmother's half-birthday,' he said to lighten the mood, but then winced and tried to take her in his arms.

Romy stepped back. 'That was before I found out you had a wife and child. You are assuming a lot,' she hissed under her breath.

Luca closed his eyes for a moment. He hadn't expected to have to introduce his current partner and the mother of his child in a pub after an impromptu meal. He'd blurted out the girlfriend thing because she hadn't censored it last time they'd spoken about it. She also hadn't fully agreed, he realised.

'Matteo is going home tomorrow, so he's with me tonight while Bianca and Guiseppe go out. Come round and spend time with us both?' he pleaded and hated how needy he sounded, so he squared his shoulders and tried to act nonchalant.

'I can't,' she responded. 'I'm... doing a stock check and then going to see Maya and Noah.'

Luca tried to deflect the sucker punch to his stomach,

because she'd usually have invited him along too, then he remembered his son.

'Tomorrow?' he asked as she moved past him to leave.

'Maybe...' she called behind her as she went to give a quick wave to Matteo and Bianca, and left him to walk back to the table alone.

Chapter 26

'Stop pacing,' said Maya. 'You're going to have to tell him.'

Romy halted in her tracks and turned to face her. 'I know,' she snapped, and then regretted it. 'Sorry.'

She hung her head and Maya guided her to a table and sat her down. 'I'll make us some tea.'

This seemed to be Maya's answer to everything lately, now that they wouldn't open a bottle of wine and drink the lot.

Romy picked up her phone to see how long they had before she needed to open the Wildlife Tearoom. She'd come in early to check on the birds. Normally she enjoyed the quiet time before the rest of the river was awake but now she tried not to keep glancing across the water to Luca's cruise liners.

She looked down glumly at her dark green Converse trainers. She wondered if her ankles would start to swell with the pregnancy and she'd have to live in flip-flops over the winter. The baby was due at the end of December, and it was now mid-

July. Her baby was three and a half months old, and her tummy was beginning to show a small bump. She looked at it incredulously each morning and spoke softly to her child all the time. To Clara, she probably seemed like a crazy lady always muttering to herself, so lately Romy had been avoiding her.

Sunlight filtered through the windows and danced across the wooden floor of the tearoom. Romy was wearing jeans and a short-sleeved T-shirt that didn't hug her middle, even though she was barely showing. She'd become paranoid about bumping her stomach and took her vitamins religiously.

'You look tired,' Maya noted, handing her the tea and a couple of slices of toast.

Romy smiled at the plate, as her sister didn't normally cook. 'Thanks! You learnt to make toast when you covered for me here, then?' she asked as she bit into the slightly burnt offering. Maya had slathered it with butter and marmalade, so Romy wasn't complaining. Maya gently swatted her sister's shoulder with the tea towel she was holding and then sat down opposite her. She gave Romy a stare and she caved.

'I'm still reeling from what Aaron told me. One minute I think I can't have children, and then next I find out I'm three months pregnant!'

'It's been a lot,' agreed Maya, her tone sympathetic. 'Have you spoken to Aaron since? Arthur threatened to ruin his life if he upset you again.'

'Well, he clearly ignored Arthur. Please don't let on, though,' she pleaded. 'Aaron keeps texting me and he's tried calling but I've blocked his number now. He even sent me flowers professing his love. I gave them to the swan sanctuary to put in their reception.'

'How are things going there?' Maya changed tack and Romy was grateful.

'Great! I love it. They call me when a new bird is brought in and I'm there most weeks checking the ones they already have. They used to face astronomical vet's fees. Now they just pay for the medicines.'

'Surely you charge them for your expertise?' Maya was horrified.

Romy's eyes sparkled. 'No. It's a charity and they struggle as it is. The work they do there is amazing, Maya. You must come and see. I enjoy it there. I feel useful.'

'I can see that. I'd love to visit,' Maya answered. 'And I'm glad to see you smiling at last, but how can you continue with that work and a baby? You own a tearoom!'

'I don't know,' Romy said honestly. 'The whole thing has been such a shock. For now, I'm enjoying my own space and getting my head round the fact that there is a baby in my future.'

'I'm so proud of the beautiful business you've created here, with the tearoom. It's a viable concern now. It's so you! Will you sell it?' Maya asked, looking around at the hard-working wooden tables and functional but super-comfortable chairs. Each had pale blue cushions with images of ducks and swans swimming on them.

Romy wasn't usually a homemaker, but she'd begun to bring in little touches that reflected the water and the birds on the boat. Some of Maya's stunning watercolour scenes of the Thames hung on the walls, too. The most recent one featured the plants around the tea boat, including Himalayan balsam, with its bright pink flowers, and great willowherb, with its tall stems and delicate white-centred pink flowers. The paintings always made Romy smile, even when she was tired after a long stint in the tearoom.

'Thanks,' Romy answered her sister's praise and felt her skin grow warm. Her sister was always telling her she was brilliant, but Romy basked in the moment. Maya was only three years older than her, but she had been mothering her for years. After their parents had left them with their grand-parents, they'd huddled together for strength. Maya's protective streak hadn't always hit the mark and there had been squabbles, but her heart was in the right place and Romy knew Maya would also tell her if she ever thought she was wrong. She'd definitely voiced her reservations when Romy dropped her vet's practice and bought a houseboat tearoom, but she'd also understood in the end.

'I definitely won't sell the boat,' Romy continued. 'I love this place. It's my home. I know I live with Clara, but that's going to become more difficult. I've been clearing out the storerooms downstairs again so that I can move back here if I need to.'

Maya's mouth dropped open in alarm. 'You can't bring up a baby here!'

'Of course I can. I'll build more guardrails when he or she can walk. It might not be ideal, but I can make it work.'

'Move in with Noah and me,' Maya pressed her.

Romy loved Maya, but she certainly didn't want to live with her again. She was a neat freak and she'd be forever following Romy around with a dustpan in case she dropped biscuit crumbs on the spotless floor. Noah was just as bad.

'That's so kind of you, but I like living alone.'

'You won't be alone soon,' her sister commented archly, and Romy rubbed her tummy.

'Are you in pain?' Maya jumped up and bent to look at Romy's tummy, which made her laugh.

'Are you going to heal me by looking at my stomach?' she grinned.

Maya chuckled and rested her head on Romy's tummy for a moment. 'I don't know. I thought I might be able to see if something was wrong,' she laughed. 'Not that I'm an expert,' she added quietly.

Romy sat up straight and her sister almost fell over.

'Do you want a baby?' Romy couldn't hide the excitement in her tone.

'I don't know,' Maya admitted. 'But it's something we've started to talk about. Noah's even mentioned marriage in passing.'

Romy jumped up and squealed. 'Marriage! Babies!' She danced around and Maya laughed.

'Nothing's decided yet, but we might plan a Christmas wedding next year,' she admitted. 'He just needs to ask me properly first!'

'Oh Maya. I'm so happy for you,' Romy said, tears springing to her eyes.

'You don't need to cry about it,' Maya teased with a wide smile.

'Happens all the time at the moment,' Romy admitted as she started to clear away the cups and plates and scan the room to make sure the tearoom was ready for opening time, which was in ten minutes. Maya reached over and gave her a hug. Then Romy looked across the water to Luca's boats, like she did about a thousand times a day.

'Tell him,' Maya said, steel in her tone.

'I will,' Romy replied. 'He just has to finish saying goodbye to his ex-wife, who I'm pretty sure thinks she has first dibs for life, and his son. He misses him like crazy when he's not here.'

'I still can't believe she did that to him,' Maya raged, her fists bunching as she reached the door.

'I know. Me neither.'

Romy wasn't sure she should have told Maya about Luca's past, but it seemed to her that most of his staff knew anyway, so it wasn't exactly a secret. It was just something he'd kept from her, which made her furious. She knew she had to keep calm for her baby's sake, but the more she thought about the way Luca had treated her, the more it was becoming mixed up with her resentment at Aaron.

Supposing she hadn't wanted a baby now? What would she have done then? Aaron left her thinking she couldn't get pregnant and that was why she'd had a miss-step with Luca, not that she'd ever regret it. She wasn't usually so irresponsible, but never in her wildest dreams had she thought that a rampant sex session without protection would result in a baby. It wasn't that she didn't usually use protection, she most certainly did. It was just that Luca had got past her usual very strict rules and she'd thought she couldn't have children! She felt stupid, and now she was living with the consequences. She was a grown woman, for goodness sake, she could have resisted the charms of Luca Bowen... then she sighed, as she knew she was lying to herself.

Romy slapped on a smile as her first customer of the day strolled onto the deck and sat at his usual table. Clint always walked along the river with his old German Shepherd dog early in the morning and he stopped for her strongest coffee and thick buttery toast most days. Romy waved to show she'd seen him and started up her coffee machine. The problem was that she didn't know how to tell Luca about his second unplanned child.

Chapter 27

Luca's texts were getting crosser and crosser. He'd asked to meet Romy now that Matteo and Bianca had gone home, but she'd stalled. It had only been a few days, but he was being insistent, even after she'd asked for space.

She remembered how it had felt to be back in his arms, after their steamy kiss in the pub last week, but her hormones were all over the place. One minute she was almost ecstatic about impending motherhood, the next she was petrified it would be a disaster and was making herself sick with anxiety. She'd had to unblock Aaron and speak to him about selling their business, but she'd kept it terse and unemotional. The sale was going through and it would buffer her transition into working less for a while. In the end, she'd handed it all over to her brother Arthur to handle.

Arthur was controlling his anger at Aaron with aplomb, but she knew he'd warned him to stay away from his sister. Arthur was a genial kind of guy until you upset someone he loved, then you came up against a wall of steel. His help right now meant she could take a step back and trust he would take care of the paperwork and sever all connections to the guy who had ruined her life.

The financial windfall from the sale of her vet's practice would mean she could take on two staff members to run the tearoom, and stop falling into bed each night in an exhausted heap. Clara fussed around her, but Romy knew Clara could feel the wall she was building between them. All ties with Aaron would soon be broken. Luca clearly told lies too, so maybe she was better off without either of them?

The crushing heartbreak at losing her old life was long gone. In fact, she felt free. She didn't need to please a man and she was self-sufficient. Grabbing the coffee and toast for her customer, she went and sat with him for a minute or two. This was her favourite part of her day. Her customers' most frequently asked questions were about the river and habitats of the birds, so she felt like she was educating others about their welfare. She hadn't had much chance to work with birds at her old practice, but she felt more and more that she'd found her specialism, even if it came in the form of the Wildlife Tearoom.

'How have you been?' she asked Clint, her regular. The most charming thing about her job, apart from Bob the duck and the other birds, was the company of strangers. No one knew her well or judged her. Many had become repeat visitors, but some were just passing by, as it was such a popular town and tourist Mecca. They didn't know about Aaron, the way he'd treated her, or how messed up she'd been. They didn't know how burnt she'd been by close friends, either, and that was why she didn't have any of them now. Acquaintances were fine by her.

She did wonder what everyone would think once her baby bump began to show through her baggy clothes, as people knew she was resolutely single. Luca hadn't come to the boat during the day, even when things had been good between them, so customers wouldn't know about him unless they'd heard on the town grapevine. Most of them would be glad she was having a baby, she hoped. But if they weren't, what did she care? She was finally going to be a mother!

'All good,' Clint responded, breaking off the corner of his toast to feed the hopeful-looking German Shepherd by his leg. Romy shook her head and rolled her eyes at him.

'You know I have healthy dog treats on the boat for Billy if you want them,' she scolded gently. She couldn't help but think in veterinary terms about a dog's condition and found it hard to curb her 'tips' about wellbeing and diet. Bob the duck waddled past but Billy didn't take a jot of notice, because he was used to him. She quickly went inside and returned with a glass jar of homemade peanut butter and carrot bone-shaped dog treats and offered one to Billy, with his owner's consent.

'That duck is taking his life in his hands most days,' Clint joked, nodding towards Bob who was looking for breadcrumbs.

'Luckily, most of my customers come here because they like the birds. It keeps the dogs occupied as well. They watch them steadily,' she laughed. 'I haven't had one try and grab a mallard yet!'

'Bob is becoming a bit of local celebrity. I saw a piece about this place in the paper.'

Romy chuckled at that. 'I know. It was about the rebranded tearoom, but Bob took centre stage as usual! I'm thinking of setting up his own social media page,' she said.

She jumped up as more customers began to fill the tearoom. Bob stuck his head around the door sometime later and she grinned and scooped some birdseed into her palm to scatter black sunflower seeds mixed with oats on the roof for him. He waddled along behind her and she was glad to see his tail feathers were growing back.

The day had been filled with camaraderie and easy-going chit-chat. She would be at the swan sanctuary for a few hours the next day. At least she didn't have to worry about bumping into Luca while she was there, or the fiery Italian bursting a blood vessel when she finally admitted she was carrying his child.

Chapter 28

The door opened and Clara looked up and smiled at her grandson. His grin wasn't as bright as usual and he had bags under his eyes. She gestured for him to come and sit opposite her at the breakfast bar while she chopped up some vegetables.

'You ok?' she asked, handing him some sliced carrots to snack on. He picked up a baton and then put it down again.

'I'm not sure,' he answered honestly.

'Missing Matteo?' She turned and filled the kettle with water and then brought out two mugs and some tea bags while the kettle boiled. Then she clearly changed her mind and made them both a huge gin and tonic, which he sipped gratefully.

'I always miss him, but I have to tough it out.'

Clara rested her hand on his for a moment and then came round and gave him a hug. She was half his size, but she gave great cuddles, so he stayed that way for a moment and indulged in feeling calm for a second. He had been floundering recently, when he liked to be in control.

She let him go and asked him to follow her outside. The

sun was still blazing in the sky, even though it was six o'clock. They settled at her little metal table and chairs outside the back door. He knew this was her favourite place, because she could watch the world go by on the river and not have to get involved. There wasn't much activity on the water this evening, as most people headed home after a long day, or went to get some dinner in the array of restaurants that lined the road up towards the castle.

'You can ask for help,' she told him. 'You don't always need to manage everything on your own. How's things with you and Romy?' she asked pertly. He shrugged and she took his hand. 'I wish I could make things better for you, instead of worse.'

She wouldn't meet his eye for a moment and his stomach flipped over. Could this day get any worse? He'd already shouted at an innocent staff member and had a rollicking from his brother about it.

'What do you mean?' he asked, though he wasn't sure he wanted the answer. 'She wants space, but I'm struggling to give that to her.'

'You're in love,' Clara said wisely.

He didn't argue with her. 'Is something wrong?' Luca frowned. 'You seem tense.'

'I need to tell you something.' Clara gazed out at the river, and now his stomach began swirling in earnest. He had a bad feeling this "something" was about him and Romy, or even worse, Romy and Aaron. 'I don't know how you are going to react.'

'Tell me,' he sighed, rubbing the back of his neck. He tried to straighten his shoulders, but he was exhausted.

Luca had seen the flowers from Aaron professing his love, and from that it was easy to surmise he and Romy could be back together. Now the look on his *nonna*'s face told him her news was about to shatter his world. Luca's heart sank. His fists bunched, but he refrained from jumping up and pacing back and forth. He needed to hear *Nonna* out. And he wouldn't let that guy win. Aaron didn't deserve a woman like Romy. Then the realisation hit Luca that he had lied to her too, and been presumptuous with her feelings, so he might not be what she needed either.

'Romy hasn't been herself lately and I've heard her being sick,' Clara told him. 'At first, I was worried that she was unwell... then I saw the special vitamins.'

Luca scratched his head in bewilderment. Was Romy still ill?

'Maya has been hovering around like a lost puppy,' his *nonna* continued. 'I'm pretty sure no one else knows about it yet and I haven't wanted to confront Romy, but I have to put you first.'

'Knows about what?' Luca asked. 'What does Maya know that I don't?'

'Romy's pregnant.'

'She's pregnant...' he repeated woodenly. 'What?' Romy was pregnant? This time he did jump up in alarm.

Clara caught his hand and stilled him. 'She's been avoiding me, but I can tell. She's changed how she behaves and she's wearing baggy clothes.'

Luca scoffed, his pulse calming a little. Was that it? 'Romy always wears whatever is most comfortable. She doesn't care about fashion!' His *nonna* could be a drama queen at times, but this was ridiculous. 'She can't have children,' he added quietly, sitting down again.

'She can now,' Clara said.

'What do you mean?'

'I told you, there were pregnancy vitamins on her bedside table. She's put them away now but I saw them when I went into her room to collect a water glass. She's also hardly been eating.'

'But... but...'

'I know.'

Luca thought back to the times they'd been reckless. She'd said they were safe. He'd assumed she was on birth control but hadn't taken the time to clarify. They'd used condoms ever since. Surely it couldn't happen that easily? Some of his friends had been trying for months, even years, for a baby.

'Is she back with Aaron?' he ground out, his heart racing, his teeth grinding.

'Luca, no!'

'He sent her flowers,' he added grumpily.

'And she promptly threw them in the bin. I rescued them and told her to donate them to the swan sanctuary reception, where they could brighten someone else's day.'

Luca glowered at her but she ignored that. She took his hands in her own. 'Something has definitely happened with Aaron, but she'd never go back there, I'm sure. She clearly hates him.'

'But I upset her. I told Matteo she was my girlfriend without asking her first. I told Bianca too.'

'You told Bianca that Romy was your girlfriend?' Clara sat back in her chair, astonishment on her face. Then a slow smile spread across it and her eyes sparkled. 'Bravo!'

'Romy wasn't so impressed. I upset her. She was annoyed. Maybe she did something with Aaron and then regretted it?'

'I'm pretty sure she wouldn't let that man anywhere near her romantically. He hurt her pretty badly, from what she told me when we first met. Could the baby be yours?'

His silence answered her question.

'Oh Luca!' she tried to hide her delight, but couldn't. 'A new grandchild! A brother or sister for Matteo!'

'We don't know that. I can't go through this again.'

'You don't have to,' Clara said firmly. 'Romy is not Bianca.'

'I didn't think Bianca was capable of treating me that way until she did. We'd been together since we were nineteen!'

Luca banged his fists on the table and stood up, making his gin and tonic glass tip over, spilling liquid through the scrolled metal flowered design of the table and onto the grass as he reached out and caught it. Luckily the glass didn't break, but he felt his heart split in two. Clara straightened the glass up and came round to give her grandson a hug.

He felt tears welling up in his eyes and brushed them away. History was repeating itself. There was no way he'd bring up another child not knowing if it was his. Why hadn't Romy told him earlier? The only reason he could think of was because the child wasn't his.

Chapter 29

Hauling herself out of bed on time to open the café was getting harder and harder. Romy had given herself a stern talking-to the night before, about how showing vulnerability was ok.

She had made a decision too. She would show Luca that she loved him, and was trying to work out how best to do that. She'd thought of cooking him a meal the way he had for her. It seemed like eons ago, but it was literally only a couple of months. Another idea she'd scribbled on a notepad was to invite him round when Clara was out and stand there, stark naked. He'd immediately see the changes to her body that way. But she was a bit too bashful about making quite such a bold statement. The third was to answer his texts and arrange to talk. The problem was that over the past few days his messages had dwindled to nothing. He'd given a few terse replies to her tentative texts. Where was that fiery Luca who would fight the world for her?

How did you tell the guy you were dating that you were carrying his child, when you were a complete mess at relationships? Maya made it sound so easy, but she wasn't the one who had to tell an angry Italian sex god that she was having his baby. Romy craved his touch, but she was also scared that the changes to her body might turn him off. He'd been through this with Bianca, but that baby hadn't been his. How had he behaved around her when he'd still thought Matteo was his child?

All of these questions and more flowed through her body until she couldn't sleep, and huge bags appeared under her eyes. She must look like a hag, she feared. She'd probably scare him away with her unkempt hair and wide eyes. Needing a shower and another stern talking-to, she was worried about scaring customers with her appearance.

As she walked into the kitchen, Clara glanced up from the small pull-along suitcase she was zipping shut. 'What's happening?' asked Romy and Clara stood up and then came and hugged her, rather hard!

'I didn't quite know how to tell you, but Henry has asked me to move in with him.'

'What? What the hell is going on with the world? When was this decided?'

Clara took Romy's hand and led her to sit on one of the stools by the breakfast bar, while she made her a cup of tea.

'He asked me last night, and I'm too old for playing games.'

Romy frowned and then sighed heavily. She didn't know if she could cope with much more change, but she would have to fess up to Clara and move out at some point soon anyway. The problem was – where the hell would she live now? She'd got bored clearing out the tearoom stores, and besides everything exhausted her these days. Long hours on her feet at the Wildlife Tearoom were making her feet swell and she was a bit worried about carrying trays laden with too many hot drinks now as well. She had good arm muscles, but she felt worn out.

'I didn't realise it was that kind of relationship. Well... I'd suspected by the constant text conversations and late-night phone calls,' Romy's eyes sparkled at last. She was happy for Clara... she was! Her landlady certainly had a more exciting love life than Romy did, it seemed. Clara chuckled and handed Romy the steaming cup of tea, which she sipped gratefully.

'He's a kind man and his flat has a sea view that's spectacular. You and Luca must visit.'

'Um... I'm not sure that will happen, but thanks anyway.'

Clara gave her a mysterious smile and drank her own coffee, which was strong and pungent. Romy usually loved the slightly bitter aroma of the strong coffee Clara favoured, but recently it made her feel queasy.

'What will happen to the bungalow? What about my mooring?' Romy blurted out suddenly, while she tried to warm her hands around the tea mug. The sun was already streaming through the windows and lighting up the room, but it was early and it hadn't heated the floor yet. 'Sorry. It might not be a good time to ask, but are you coming back?'

'I'm not sure,' Clara answered honestly. 'I think it's time for change – for all of us.' She gave Romy a hard stare.

Romy gulped. 'You want me to move out?'

'Of course not! But Luca is moving back in,' she added hastily, as she rinsed her mug out in the sink and left it on the drainer.

'What? Um... what?' Romy blinked and she was sure Clara had just said Luca was moving back in? He lived in Mayfair. 'What did you just say?' she repeated.

Clara gave her a gentler hug and then wheeled her suitcase to the door. Romy trailed after her helplessly. 'What about all your stuff? I'm so confused. What do you mean Luca is moving back in?'

'She means I'm moving back in.' said Luca simply as she gasped. He was standing in the doorway.

Romy's eyes feasted on him and then she felt her cheeks flush and looked away.

'But... You haven't been answering my messages,' she knew she sounded whiny. She realised she was still wearing her pyjama shorts set and her hair was messy. She self-consciously ran her fingers through it, but it didn't really help.

Luca was wearing slim fitting jeans that clung to his leg muscles lovingly and that dratted black short sleeved Bowen Brothers work shirt that made her insides all squirmy. Her mouth watered and she was lost for words for a moment. He had a huge case with him, which he stored by the door.

'It seems we have something to talk about?' he raised an eyebrow at her and fire raged in his eyes.

Romy took a step back. She glanced at Clara who shrugged in apology, and Romy understood that they both knew. Her skin grew hot and she hung her head. Luca hugged his grandmother and Henry honked his car horn as he pulled into the driveway. Luca carried her case out to the car as Clara and Romy said their goodbyes.

'He knows? You know?' she asked Clara.

'I had to tell him. I'm sorry,' replied Clara. 'I saw the vitamins.'

Romy grimaced and realised she should have been more careful. Clara didn't come into her room very often, though, so she must have spotted them that first morning when Maya gave them to her.

'I'm sorry. I didn't know how to tell him, or you.'

'You don't need to apologise to me,' Clara hugged her again and Romy sank into it. 'He might be another matter, though.' She took Romy's hands for a moment. 'Can I ask something of you?'

'Anything.'

'Luca's hurt. He's angry. He might say things he doesn't mean. Remember that he loves you.' Romy gulped and stepped back, but nodded her head.

This was her worst nightmare. In the past, she'd imagined telling the father of her child about their impending exciting news, but the picture had only ever been of Aaron. Now Luca had exploded into every aspect of her life and taken over. He was moving back in! She'd have to move out.

Chapter 30

'm pregnant,' Romy blurted out as soon as Luca had come back and shut the door behind him. His eyes were dark and angry and his mouth was set in a hard line. This hadn't been how she'd planned to tell him, but standing starkers seemed like completely the wrong tack right now.

'Is it mine?' he ground out as he got closer and stood right in front of her. Her eyes went wide in shock and her own fists clenched.

'What? Who the hell else's could it be?'

'Aaron's? I saw the huge bunch of flowers saying how much he loved you. Plus the texts, for weeks and weeks, after we began dating. Were you seeing him again then? Our relationship wasn't exactly planned,' he shrugged, but his face was set and angry.

Romy raised a hand to strike him but he caught her wrist in his and moved closer so that they were chest to chest. Hers was rising and falling at a rapid rate and she went to kick him, but he pulled her into his arms and kissed her as if he was dying. Tears filled her eyes as her hands wound around him and into his hair. Then she let go and pushed hard at his chest so that he dropped his arms. Both of their eyes were filled with sadness as they stepped apart.

'I haven't been anywhere near Aaron for years. I promise you,' she added.

'The texts? Flowers? You went out for dinner with him and things haven't been the same between us since.'

'You think I was sleeping with both of you back then?' she demanded to know. He flinched but didn't answer. 'I told you how much I loathe that man. The only reason I speak to him now is to finalise the sale of our business. If I never saw him again it would be too soon.'

'Will you do a paternity test?'

Romy crouched over as if he'd punched her, and he quickly picked her up in his arms and gently placed her on the sofa. Pictures of the number of times they'd begun to make love there filled her mind, as did the red mist of rage.

She sat up and then stood, staring him straight in the eye, but he refused to back down and was standing as rigidly as she was now.

'You wouldn't do that to Bianca, but you will now? You know I haven't slept with anyone but you.'

'Romy,' he rubbed his eyes and stepped back. 'You have to understand my reasons.'

Then he changed tack and tried to reach out to her, but she stomped back to her room and slammed the door shut behind her. She stripped off her top just as the door swung open again. She gasped and clasped her hands over her chest, but he was immobilised by the sight of her softly rounded belly.

'Haven't you heard of knocking!' she said, anger and embarrassment lacing her voice.

'This is my room too now,' he said reasonably as he took a step nearer, but her eyes warned him to stop.

'Clara has moved out, so her room is now yours. If you think for one moment I'm sharing a bed with a man who thinks I'd cheat on him after all I've been through, then you don't know me at all.'

His eyes darkened to an even deeper shade of brown and he flushed. 'You know my reasoning.'

'I do. I just don't understand it. I am not Bianca,' she reiterated. 'I would never do that to you.'

'That's what she said too,' he said sadly, as he backed out of the room and she hastily shoved on some clothes and ran into the bathroom to get ready for work.

This day certainly wasn't panning out the way she'd envisaged when she'd woken up. Not only did she now need to find a new home and possibly a new mooring for her business, but she had a sexy Italian problem back in the cottage. Now that they were having a child together, their lives would be bound together forever, just not in the way she'd secretly hoped and dreamed of for months now.

She didn't have time to worry anymore because it was getting towards opening time and she needed to rush to get the boat ready. So much for some quiet time before her first customers of the day arrived. She pulled on her jeans, leaving the top two buttons undone, and slipped her arms into the new branded top she'd ordered in a larger size, even though she was barely showing yet. She tried to let her problems drift away and enjoy the sun on her face as she hastily walked up the garden path to the Wildlife Tearoom. She stopped and stared at it for a moment and pride swelled in her chest. Not so long ago she'd thought she was unable to put one foot in front of the other, but now people were already hovering around outside her very popular floating tearoom and enjoying the view of the water and the birds on her roof.

She had despaired of having a child for so long that she'd almost shut away the part of her brain that believed it might ever happen. Now here she was, an entrepreneur and a mother-to-be. It might not be the exact way she'd envisaged this happening, but she'd got there on her own. Well, almost on her own... with a little help from the most annoying man on the planet. She flinched when she thought about him asking her for a paternity test. She did understand why, but wished with all her heart that he loved her enough to believe her. She guessed he'd loved Bianca more.

She waved to two dog walkers who often stopped by for coffee and cupcakes and opened up the boat. She always felt like the boat gave her a warm hug of welcome and she didn't want to think about moving. The location, right by Clara's bungalow, was perfect. A short stroll across the bridge which linked both sides of the river led straight up to the pretty cobbled streets of the town and its stone and brick fronted shops. It also led to Luca and Alex's cruises and to *Bertha*, the only steamboat on this stretch of the river.

Maybe Romy needed a day off and a cruise on *Bertha*? She certainly wouldn't be travelling on a Bowen boat any time soon. She cursed because every thought led back to that grumpy Italian. She caught sight of him talking to a group of customers and heard a tinkly laugh from one woman as she touched his arm to get his attention. Romy grimaced as he looked up and their eyes met. She swore under her breath at being caught staring. She'd just popped out on deck to feed the birds and check the outside of the boat was clean. A local lad called Connor arrived every other day to wash down the outside of the boat and clean the areas the birds used, and it always looked pristine.

Romy groaned inside as she looked up and saw her grandmother, Ettie, walking up the pathway from the promenade. She gave a quick smile, then ducked into the boat to take her next order. The noise caused by blasting the milk with hot air to make it frothy kept her grandmother from talking for a moment. Romy expertly made four fragrant coffees and waited for the teacakes that had been ordered to pop up from her industrial toaster. She added little ramekins of thick creamy butter to each plate and then handed two to her grandmother to assist, which put off the questions that Romy knew instinctively were coming. How did everyone suddenly know she was pregnant?

When she finally had a moment to sit with her grandmother, she admired her beautifully embroidered long summer shirt, with bursts of tiny white elderflowers sewn all over it. She'd matched it with taupe linen trousers, which had a slightly darker tone, and velvet piping down the sides. Being a designer to the stars, Ettie always dressed stylishly and Romy loved seeing her latest work. Often they would end up being worn by celebrities or royals when Ettie decided to make something new. She was supposed to be retired, but seemed busier than ever to Romy.

Ettie sipped her coffee patiently while Romy fussed about, and then finally gave her a hard stare to stop her fidgeting. They were at the table nearest the kitchen, so no one else could hear them, but Romy still glanced around her surreptitiously.

'So?' Ettie asked.

'How did you find out?' Romy said quietly.

'Your sister caved. She's worried about you. I'm sad you didn't tell me yourself.'

Romy sniffed and her eyes became glassy. 'I'm sorry.' She hung her head, and her grandmother took her hand. 'I wanted to, but thought I should tell Luca first. Maya only found out because my tummy was hurting.'

'She told me about that, too. Have you called your parents?'

'No,' Romy sighed, quickly looking up to make sure her customers had everything they needed. It was the lull before the lunchtime rush, and she was tempted to slip her trainers off and wriggle her toes because her feet were aching. 'I'm going to tell them tonight. It still doesn't feel real. What if something goes wrong?'

'It won't,' assured her grandmother. 'You're strong and healthy and you've been dreaming of this moment for years, so I'm sure you're doing everything in your power to protect my first great-grandchild.'

'Of course I am!'

'You need new staff.'

'I know, but I'm managing for now. As soon as the vet's practice is sold, I've got two new staff starting.'

'I could help,' Ettie offered.

'Umm... thank you, but I can manage.'

Romy's grandparents brought chaos wherever they went, because they were so well known. The few customers Romy had today were already peeking at Ettie over the rim of their drinks when she wasn't looking. Her grandad was worse, now that he had his own television show about rare plants. He had a huge fan base, which Ettie found hilarious!

'Then let me book you a temporary waitress until your permanent staff start? Please, Romy. We are all concerned about you.'

Romy baulked at her family's interference, but then her shoulders sagged. She needed to learn to accept help when it was offered. It would be good to have another pair of hands in the tearoom.

'Ok, thank you,' Romy said. Her grandmother's eyebrows shot into her hairline and then she coughed and composed herself. 'I know. I'm stubborn. But I have to put my baby first.'

'How did Luca take it?' Ettie was aware of Matteo and Luca's history with Bianca, now, so this was a delicate subject for everyone.

'He asked me to take a paternity test,' replied Romy, and Ettie flinched.

'He has been through a lot,' her grandmother said.

'I know, but it made me so mad! He didn't ask Bianca,' Romy said crossly.

'Look how that worked out,' said her grandmother gently and Romy flushed.

'I had already asked the doctor for one because I didn't want Luca to have the slightest doubt this time. I guessed he wouldn't ever totally relax without one. I just didn't tell Luca that. It's so embarrassing – as if I don't know who the father of my child is, when I do.'

'So, tell him.'

Romy gave her gran a mutinous look, and she ignored it. 'Did Maya tell you about Aaron as well? I said she could, about that part.'

'The less we speak *his* name the better,' Ettie seethed, and Romy raised a smile finally. 'I want to smack his legs with my walking stick.'

'You don't use a walking stick! You threw out that old one of grandad's.'

'I'll buy one,' Ettie grinned suddenly and her eyes sparkled. 'Your new staff member needs to start soon, so find someone quickly.'

'I thought you'd already have someone lined up?' chuckled Romy, and then she froze. 'Gran! You do.'

'Well. A friend's granddaughter is at home from uni for the summer and she's studying catering. It would help her to have work experience in the industry, so she can put it on her CV. Her name's Saffron. She's already a customer of yours and comes in regularly. She's very excited.'

'Gran!'

'She's outside...'

'Honestly!' Romy threw her hands in the air in resignation. 'She's been sitting outside all this time? Bring her in.'

Ettie grinned and stepped onto the deck, returning with Saffron, whom Romy already knew quite well by sight.

'Saffron! I'm sorry Gran made you wait outside. I had no idea,' said Romy.

Saffron flushed as red as her long hair and didn't know where to look. 'Is this ok?' she asked, with a worried frown. 'I wasn't sure. Ettie said it was going to be a surprise, but I'm not sure that works when you're applying for a job.'

Romy chuckled again and shook her head. 'Nothing is done the way it should be in my family, but I'm very glad to have you here. You've worked in cafés before, haven't you, if I remember rightly?'

'Yes,' Saffron smiled as she whipped a hairband out and pulled her hair into a tight ponytail. 'I worked at the pub across the water for about six months and also the café on my university campus.'

'Perfect. Well, you might as well start now, if that works. Grab an apron and bring in any used plates and cutlery from outside.'

Saffron gave her a wide grin and turned around immediately, grabbing a tray on the way to put empty glasses on. Romy let out a sigh of relief and leaned in to hug her gran.

'Thank you.'

'Tell Luca,' Ettie said over her shoulder as she left the coffee shop and said a quick hello to a few acquaintances as she passed.

'I'll try,' mumbled Romy under her breath, but couldn't imagine a good time to mention something like having already taken a paternity test, when they were always arguing.

Maybe she'd take home some cake tonight and try to bring it up? Then she squashed that idea because she just didn't know if Luca was happy about the fact he was becoming a father again. He certainly hadn't told her so, and jealousy at Bianca having a doting partner when she was pregnant reared its ugly head. For all Romy knew, Luca was out most nights on dates with different women, so he should hardly be asking her about paternity when he was far from an angel himself.

She huffed and stomped into the kitchen to prepare for the lunchtime rush. Pushing away thoughts of Luca wrapped in the arms of the stylish, laughing brunette from earlier that day wasn't easy. In the end, she channelled the energy into slicing cucumbers rather aggressively and then sighed and decided to get a life.

Chapter 31

Luca had tried to get home early to see Romy and hash everything out, but there had been an issue with the hull of the boat. It had struck a tree trunk that had fallen into the river. It wasn't a huge problem for a boat that size, and the tree had broken up, but Luca was a perfectionist and he'd insisted getting into one of their speedboats and checking the hull of the boat for damage when they had returned to dock.

Crowds of people had filled their boats that day and he'd had two staff members off sick, which meant both he and Alex had to step in and cover their work too. His shoulders ached and he needed a glass of wine. He paused outside the back door of his *nonna*'s house and tried to calm his heart rate. He hated arguing with Romy, but it seemed to be part of their relationship. Not that he was allowed to call it a relationship, of course. He knew he shouldn't have asked her for a paternity test the moment he'd said it, but he'd been angry at her for keeping the fact that she was pregnant from him. He felt as if she'd stolen that moment of joy at having his own biological child, and giving Matteo a brother or sister.

Concentrating had been hard all day, which was why he hadn't managed to dodge the tree in the river. Normally he'd just have waited for it to drift by, but he'd practically sliced it in half! Luckily his customers hadn't noticed but Alex had riled him up about it. He was going to be a dad, but the small niggle that Aaron had managed to worm his way into Romy's affections again scared the hell out of him. He couldn't live through a situation like that twice. It had destroyed him last time.

He stepped inside, but there was an eerie quiet. He shut the door behind him and walked around looking for Romy. He found her fast asleep on their bed, her blonde hair fanning out on the covers and her dark eyelashes brushing her cheek. She'd definitely changed since he'd last lived here. Her figure was still firm and strong, but it had a softness about it and her cheeks were flushed in slumber. He tenderly brushed a stray hair out of her eyes and her eyes fluttered open and focused on him. She didn't smile and he couldn't help himself from leaning in and touching his lips to hers.

She held back for a moment and then her arms wound around his neck and pulled him down next to her. He groaned and deepened the kiss, which made her whimper, almost sending him over the edge. They lay side by side and his hand slipped under her T-shirt and cupped her tender breasts in his hands. They felt fuller and he gently massaged her bare nipples, catching one in his mouth and feasting on her until she pushed her core towards him and her own hands slid into the back of his jeans, touching his taut backside and urging him closer. He lost all reason as he stripped her clothes from her body and kicked off his own jeans. He was loath to break contact with her, so he kept one hand on her body at all times and then they were naked and his eyes and hands roamed all over her soft skin until she was pliant in his arms.

He kissed his way down her body, but she wound her legs around his back and they rocked together in ecstasy. He'd wanted to take his time, worship her, but his mind and body had other ideas and he tried to be as gentle as he could when his body craved her like a drug. Their skin was slick together and he rained kisses all over her face and body and slid his fingers between them and touched her core until they both collapsed on the bed, replete and satisfied.

'I've missed you,' he said into the curve of her neck as he held her close.

'I'm still annoyed with you,' she sighed, but she cupped his chin and kissed his lips again, making him want more.

'I know.' He ran his hands over her gently rounded stomach in wonder and her skin flushed and she tried to turn away. 'I want to see all of you,' he said as he captured her face for another kiss. Would he ever stop wanting to kiss this woman? He doubted it.

'I don't know how to feel about all of this,' she admitted and his heart broke a little.

'I know I love you,' he said,

She sat up and pulled the duvet up to cover her body in a slightly defensive mood. So, she still didn't love him back then... he rolled over and pulled on his jeans and T-shirt, his shoulders sagging in defeat.

'Do you? You don't trust me.'

'I'm trying to,' he admitted, sitting down on the bed next to her. 'Do you want this baby?' he needed to know and she covered her mouth in horror.

'It's all I've ever wanted.'

'With Aaron.' He wished he hadn't said the words the minute they left his mouth.

She swung her legs out of the bed and grabbed her clothes, flinging them on haphazardly.

'I'm sorry,' he apologised immediately. 'I feel like a caveman. Everything about him makes me jealous.'

She froze and looked at him, her face softening. 'You never, *ever*, have to compete with that man,' she assured him, steadily.

He took hold of her arm and tugged her to sit on his lap, but she tried to wriggle away and his body was immediately hard at the contact with her backside on his lap. 'Luca! Stop it. We literally just made love.'

Hope swelled at the word love and he began nibbling his way along the nape of her neck until she gave in and kissed him with passion and longing that shook them both. He'd never felt such all-consuming need, even when they'd been fighting, and he matched her energy touch for touch. He stood up with her in his arms and settled her on the bed, looking up at him. He quickly discarded his clothes and showed her how much he wanted her. She was only wearing knickers under her T-shirt, so he sat down on the bed and pulled her back onto his lap, facing him this time. He slid her underwear aside and she mounted him. He could see she from the flush of her skin and the sound of her hitched breathing that she was enjoying setting the pace and he released all his power to her, letting her know that whatever he had was hers. She ground her hips to his as his hands found her plump breasts once again. They both cried out as their orgasms shook around them and then she sank into his arms as he cradled her, before they both fell back onto the bed in an exhausted heap.

Sometime later he turned to watch her eyelashes flutter

against her cheek as she slept and he gently pulled the covers up and around her shoulders to make sure she stayed warm. He knew they would have to talk about their baby again at some point, but for now he was just content to have her back in his arms.

Chapter 32

The sun warmed Romy's skin as she sat at the little bistro table outside Clara's bungalow. She'd had a lovely day at work with Saffron. The girl was a complete whizz! She made sure Romy had regular breaks and brought her tea and toast to check she was eating. Saffron had three much younger siblings, so she was well versed in what small children needed – including breaks for the mother.

'Mum always forgot to rest when she was pregnant,' Saffron told Romy while she was wiping the tables after a busy day with a boat full of ravenous customers. 'When I went to university I worried about her, but she loves rushing around after us all. My siblings always ask her to bring them here, as you witnessed today.' She grinned at the memory.

Romy had looked on in wonder at how good Saffron was with her half-brother and sisters. They clearly adored her and climbed all over her, which she took in good humour. It was easy to see how much she loved them too and it was probably why she was adept at multi-tasking and listening to direction.

Romy was incredibly thankful to her grandmother for having the genius idea of asking Saffron to work at the tea boat. It scared her sometimes to think how she'd managed before. She had been really silly not to have asked for help, and the thought that it might have put her unborn child in danger horrified her. She knew pregnant mothers could do pretty much anything they set their mind to, but her back had been aching and she definitely didn't want another telling off from the doctor if she got pelvic pains again. The wrath of her sister wouldn't be much fun either. Maya was already clucking around her like a mother hen.

They often had time to relax for half an hour between the morning and lunchtime rushes, so Romy now took full advantage of this for herself and her staff. 'Was it hard when you were growing up, with you having a different dad from your brothers and sisters?' she asked Saffron.

'Not really. My dad is great, he's just not the right fit for my mum. She's a lot happier now and Dad has a new partner too. It's bedlam when we are all together as he's got two other kids now too, but we love it. I was an only child for ages and now I have a huge family.'

It was wonderful seeing Saffron's eyes sparkling with love. Romy already cared for Matteo, and hopefully he would love his little brother or sister as much as Saffron loved hers. Romy hated to think that she might be the cause of more upset in his life, but she hadn't planned this, any more than Luca had.

She sighed and pushed her shoes off, wriggling her toes in the warm summer air. Luca had made her dinner the night before and they half-talked about the practicalities of having a child together, but they had steered away from anything deeper for some reason. She could tell he was still holding back.

She had received the paternity test results the day before. She hadn't bothered opening them because she knew the result, but she did understand how important it was to Luca after what he'd been through. He hadn't brought the topic up again, but she intended to. For now, she was enjoying living with him again. Making love was even better than before, if that was possible, but she'd had to remind him occasionally that she wouldn't shatter in front of him when he touched her. He was always worried about her and their child, and she kind of liked the pampering after a long day on the boat.

Romy had secretly begun nesting and had gone shopping the previous Sunday. Before that, she had stubbornly refused to believe that a miracle had happened and she was about to become a mum. Now she'd cracked, and had hidden a sage green rocker that she could nudge with her feet to help the baby snooze and had accumulated several cute newborn outfits. The pile of beautiful bibs she was collecting was getting out of hand. If she saw one with a bird design then she had to reach out and touch it, and had bought twenty so far!

Luca had discovered them and rather than shouting, he'd grinned and made her bring all her purchases out and set them on the table, so he could take it all in. She'd felt bashful at first, but he'd taken her hand and made her write out a list of things the baby would need so that they could go shopping together to get the pram, car seat and cot.

It was becoming more real with each passing day. Clicking on her phone, she scrolled some of the shopping sites she'd bookmarked to see what else she needed. She hadn't realised that she would need so much stuff! It would gradually take over the bungalow and she'd have to find a place for everything when Clara decided to come back.

Instead of feeling the fear that usually welled up at the thought of opening up to Luca, she enjoyed the warmth of knowing he had her back and whatever she or the baby needed, they would provide it together. Romy seemed to have gone from a person who didn't need much, to a mother who craved the finest of everything for her precious child. She knew he or she would probably be just as happy playing with a box of toy bricks, but she wanted her child to know how much it was loved and that this mother would never leave.

The conversation with her own parents had gone well, but they'd all had tears in their eyes by the end. It had also made Romy realise how hard it was for Luca to be away from his son, and the pain it must have caused her parents, being in a different country from their children, even if it was their choice. They saved lives, she knew that, but she had always wondered why she and her siblings hadn't been enough for them to do that here?

Chapter 33

Maya sat at a table in the pub overlooking the river. Luca had asked to meet her, but she wasn't at all sure it was a good idea. He hadn't asked her not to tell Romy, but Maya had held off, which was unusual as the sisters were each other's biggest supporters. She knew Romy had had a Zoom meeting with their parents last night, and it had ended with them all in tears. Romy had called Maya afterwards and she could tell it had been a heavy conversation.

Their parents' charity work kept them away for most of the year, but now their first grandchild was on the way, they were having a wobble. Romy had reassured them, but Maya wouldn't be surprised if they came home for a visit soon anyway. Both being doctors, they would want to check Romy's health over first hand, and reassure themselves she was ok. Who knew, they might even decide to come home. Maya would bet they got restless soon after, though a grandchild could change everything for the better. She was trying to stay open-minded about everyone's plans.

Luca arrived looking flustered and not his usual

assured self, which made Maya soften a little. She really wanted to bang both his and Romy's heads together, but she was hoping this meeting would clear a few things up. He was so tall that he nearly hit his forehead on one of the old pub's low beams and Maya smothered a laugh. He noted her and grimaced, then laughed self-deprecatingly as he tried to balance the beer and glass of Merlot he'd just bought. 'You'd never believe I was capable of running a business.'

Maya took the wine before he spilled any more, and then got up to hug him, which he sank into gratefully. 'Hard week?'

'Well, I almost capsized one of our boats,' he exaggerated, and then sighed in bliss as he sipped his cold beer. 'Plus I found out I'm going to be a dad again.'

He picked up the lunch menu then put it down again and Maya felt sorry for him suddenly.

'How do you feel about that?'

'Ecstatic... but... fearful.'

Maya took his hand and squeezed it, then quickly placed an order for a charcuterie sharing board for both of them, as Luca didn't seem to have his mind in the game.

'What are you scared of?'

'Did she go back to Aaron at any point?'

'Luca, you know she didn't,' Maya responded, her hackles rising.

'I've got so many issues,' he sighed, rubbing his hand through his hair and messing it up. 'She wouldn't even agree to be my girlfriend and now we're having a baby.'

'She wants you to trust her.'

'I'm trying. I thought I did, but *he* wants her back.'

'She doesn't want him, though,' explained Maya, as if speaking to a very small child. 'She would never, ever, go there again. She decided that years ago. She chose an annoying Italian who drives her insane.'

Luca looked up hopefully, but she could tell there was more on his mind.

'I bought her a ring, you know,' he finally said.

Maya gasped, her eyes wide. 'What?'

'Before I knew she was pregnant.'

'Why haven't you asked her?' Maya said.

'Because Matteo and Bianca turned up. We haven't been together that long, but I'm an idiot and in love. I've never felt this way before and I want her to be mine,' he shrugged, as if it was hopeless.

'Ask her,' Maya urged.

A spark of hope flickered in his eyes and then died. 'She'll think I only did it because she's pregnant.'

Maya pulled a face and took a glug of wine. This was hard work! 'You're right. She will,' she admitted, knowing her sister well. Romy was so stubborn! 'You'll just have to convince her she's wrong.'

'She's never wrong...' he shook his head and Maya's eyes crinkled at the corners in humour. Poor Luca. Romy was also argumentative.

'Plus, Aaron is still around. She won't talk about him.'

'She can't. Do you really want to know why?'

Luca nodded and sat back in his seat, as if scared by what she might say.

'He told her he'd had a vasectomy... years ago. Just after they met.'

Luca's jaw hung open and then his mouth snapped shut and his eyes filled with fire. He put his drink down and sat forward, resting his elbows on the table, which made his arm muscles bunch. This was a man ready to take someone down if they hurt her sister and Maya sat back in satisfaction. The old Luca was back.

'You're kidding me?' he raged.

'That's why she's been devastated and unresponsive. She doesn't know how to feel,' Maya explained.

'She said that, but I thought she didn't know how to feel about having our child.'

Maya sat back and regarded him. What a mess this all was. 'She's reeling. Not just because he stole her dream of being a younger mum, but for the years of invasive scans, doctors' visits and devastating news. No one could find out what was wrong. But he knew exactly why she wasn't getting pregnant – and he selfishly kept that from her!'

'I don't understand.'

'He was leaving his wife for Romy, and they had breakup sex. His wife got pregnant, and he decided to stay, but they agreed no other children for either of them.'

'He wanted his wife, and to keep Romy?' he ground out angrily and swore so loudly in Italian that the people on the table in the next room looked over.

'Sorry!' Maya apologised to them, but they just laughed. 'Aaron juggled his wife and Romy, without Romy knowing. He had four children at this point and didn't want more, so he tried to stop Romy having any at all. Although, in hindsight, I'm glad now, because it would have tied her to him forever and I hate him almost as much as she does.'

'I asked her to take a paternity test!' cried Luca, placing his head in his hands.

'You're an idiot, but we do understand. Romy understands. It just hurts that you don't trust her. She'd already booked in a paternity test before you asked for one. She put herself through the embarrassment of that for you, even though she hasn't slept with anyone else. She wanted you always to be sure. She's not Bianca.'

'I'm so sorry. I should have believed her,' he dipped his head before sitting up straight and looking at Maya. 'I wanted to marry Romy, even if the child wasn't mine. She means that much to me, and I've survived it before, but needed the truth,' he added solemnly. 'If she'd slept with Aaron just before we met, the child might have been his. I didn't know he'd had a vasectomy. It must have happened straight away for us. We were careful after that. And I know she's not Bianca.'

'You've both been through a lot,' said Maya. 'You need to talk openly to each other.' She nibbled on some bread that a server had placed on the table. 'She would never go back to Aaron. He'd hurt her too much, even before that revelation. Romy isn't a cheater and she hated the thought that she might have hurt another woman. Then it turns out Aaron's wife knew about Romy all along... not that it makes anything any better. He's still a complete git who messed up two women's lives,' Maya seethed. Luca looked just about ready to leap up and go and find her sister. 'Romy would never, ever, let you bring up another man's child without telling you the truth.'

'I know. I'm sorry,' said Luca.

'Are you? Would you have felt this way if you hadn't found out what Aaron did?'

'I would have calmed down. I was jealous,' he admitted sheepishly. 'Romy makes me feel things I haven't felt before. I want to protect her and make her happy, but she doesn't need me for any of that. She's so independent.'

'She does need you, but that excuse is not good enough,' Maya told him as their food arrived. The wooden board was packed full of cured meats, pungent cheeses and pickles.

She selected a chunky piece of seeded bread from the accompanying breadbasket and savoured her first bite after dipping it in olive oil and balsamic vinegar.

'Put your ego aside and tell her that you love her.'

'I have,' he said. 'Multiple times. She just doesn't say it back.'

Maya couldn't help but laugh at her sister's antics and decided to give the poor guy a break. 'She loves you. She's just guarding her heart. She's been hurt badly before, too. This isn't just about you.'

Luca's face paled and he stood up, then reached out to hug her. 'Are you ok here on your own?' he asked, before she tilted her head to one side and looked at him as if to say, are you stupid? He laughed and then kissed her cheek before leaving. 'Thanks, Maya. I need to go and persuade your sister to marry me.'

'Get on with it then!' she laughed back, shooing him away as he stole a piece of cured meat from the charcuterie board.

Chapter 34

Romy was suspicious. Luca was being super-nice, and he kept hovering around her as if she was a delicate little flower. Weirdly it didn't soothe her, it made her jumpy and short-tempered.

She didn't even know why he'd moved back in. Since their first night shenanigans, he was back sharing her bed but nothing more had happened between them. He seemed to think that it was ok to sleep in 'their' bed again, though, and to be honest she fell into bed exhausted most nights and woke up snuggled in his arms before she moved away. She was still annoyed at him, but he never bit back when she was snappy now and kept looking at her weirdly. It was unsettling. Arguing seemed preferable at this point. At least she knew what the hell was going on then.

She padded into the kitchen with her feet bare and didn't bother to change out of her silky pyjama shorts set. The waistband was a little bit snug now, but she hadn't had to upsize yet. She sniffed the air appreciatively and her stomach rumbled. Luca smiled at her as she approached and he placed a towering plate of freshly-cooked crumbly, buttery croissants on the table, with an open jar of jam next to it, which smelt sweet and fruity. The radio was playing smooth jazz and Sade sung *The Sweetest Taboo* in dulcet tones, making the hairs on the back of her neck stand up. Were they ever going to talk about the great big boulder blocking their relationship?

'Shall we sit outside for breakfast?' Luca suggested.

Romy's eyes narrowed at him and then she shrugged. He'd made her a fresh vegetable pasta with a heavenly cream sauce the night before but she couldn't believe how ravenously hungry she was again. She broke a piece of the croissant off and nibbled on it while he got plates out of the cupboard and loaded up the tray Clara used to take her lunch outside most days. She followed him without a word. They both had a day off that day, she knew, because he'd dropped it into conversation about a million times. He'd also made them big mugs of tea, so she picked them up and brought them with her.

'How's your new staff member working out?' he asked, pulling out a chair for her and settling her at the table, his hand brushing her shoulder as he sat next to her. She tried to concentrate on his words, but the air fizzed with sexual tension around them. This sexy man was sleeping next to her in bed each night, but suddenly he was barely touching her. Did her pregnant state put him off? She wondered suddenly. He'd treated her like a goddess when he'd first moved in. Now he was – not backing off exactly – but being weird!

'Look, that's not what you want to discuss, is it? What's this about?' she demanded to know.

'I want to apologise,' he said carefully and she noticed how tired he looked.

'I won't ask what for,' she said waspishly, them immediately regretted it because he flinched. She'd been waiting for an apology about the DNA test and she guessed this was it.

'I spoke to Maya,' he said.

Romy covered her mouth in shock and reeled back in her chair as if someone had slapped her. 'She had no right to do that!'

'I pushed her. I'm sorry.'

'So now you're sorry? Now you know the baby is yours. I did the paternity test, anyway.'

'I know. You did that for me and I'm sorry I made you feel like I don't trust you. I do. I was feeling possessive and hurt about Aaron being around. I didn't like it.' There was an edge to his voice but she disregarded it.

'Oh, for goodness sake!' she heard herself saying. For some weird reason she was very sensitive to occasional swearing now she was pregnant, when she quite enjoyed it before! Pregnancy had sent her weird, she shook her head at herself. 'I have not been near Aaron for years and would never have gone back there, even before his revelation. He cheated on me. I know lots of people can work things out after that, but he'd lied for four years. That's tough to get over, even before the vasectomy revelation. His words almost destroyed me. I had years of tests and heartbreak. I hate him for that the most.' Tears filled her eyes and she sniffed and looked away. Luca reached out a hand and placed his on hers. She didn't shake him away.

'I did the test because I don't ever want you to have a shred of doubt that this baby is yours,' she sniffed and he brushed a tear away from her cheek with the pad of his thumb. 'Even if it means embarrassing the hell out of myself by asking for a paternity test when I know who the father is. Some people don't know. That's up to them. But I'm monogamous. I've been cheated on and it hurts like hell. I'd never put another human being through that pain. If I wanted out, I'd just leave.' She felt puffed out from her outburst and her chest was heaving with emotion, her cheeks flushed.

'I know. I'm so sorry, Romy. I hated that I'd asked the moment the words left my mouth.' He rubbed the back of his neck as he leaned back in his chair, looking oh so sexy and delicious that her rampant hormones made her want to jump him, even though she currently hated him. People were beginning to mill about along the river and Romy needed to make sure Saffron had opened the boat for the day, but this couldn't wait.

'You shouldn't have needed to ask,' she said quietly, all the fire draining out of her, hanging her head as tears smarted in her eyes again.

'My past got the better of me,' he said gently.

'I'm not Bianca,' she repeated sadly. 'I wanted you not to need to ask. I wanted you to love me as much as you loved her.'

'Oh, Romy.' He came and hunched down beside her chair, his own eyes wet with tears. 'I love you more.'

'You didn't ask her.' Her bottom lip wobbled and he nudged her leg so that she had to look at him.

'I was naïve. It didn't occur to me that another human being – especially one who professed to love me – could be so cruel.'

'But you still thought I could?' Tears plopped freely onto the table now and she blinked and brushed them aside. She stood up and he clearly knew he'd lost her, as his face fell. Months of frustration filled her body and all she wanted to do was lie down.

'Romy. That's not what I meant at all. It was an involuntary reaction to the news of a new baby. I didn't mean it. I love you. You're all I've ever dreamed of in a partner, even though you still refuse to be my girlfriend,' he tried to lighten the mood. 'Having a child with you is the best thing that's ever happened to me.'

She froze and stared at him unseeingly for a moment and then her eyes filled with fresh tears because she wasn't sure she believed him anymore, so she slowly walked away into the house and left him standing alone.

Chapter 35

Luca held his head in his hands and groaned. Why did he always mess things up? Romy was the first person he'd loved in so long, but he kept getting it wrong. At least he was consistent, he thought scathingly. Waiting until he heard Romy go into the bathroom, he slid his mobile phone from his jeans pocket to make a call home. He'd already told his parents about Romy and the baby, but he really wanted to hear the sound of his mother's voice right now.

'*Pronto,*' said his mother as she answered the phone in her soft lilting Italian accent.

'*Ciao, Mamma.*'

'Luca! How are you?' He smiled at the joy in her tone every time he called, and he felt guilty that he didn't get home more often to the place he loved. Bologna was sometimes nicknamed La Rossa because of its multitude of terra-cotta tiled roofs. He felt lucky to live in Windsor now and to have Clara and Alex nearby, but his heart would always belong to his Italian roots. Vowing to visit more often, he wanted to take Romy and the baby there – if she could stand being near him for longer than five minutes.

'I messed up.'

'With Romy? Why? What happened?' his mother asked gently. She was the polar opposite of Romy, who was fiery and argumentative. Both women were caring, supportive and kind, though. 'Did you apologise?'

'I did, but it didn't work out.'

'You want us to visit?' His heart melted a little. Both his parents had busy lives, but they would still drop everything for their boys.

'Not yet,' he sighed, sitting back down at the table and letting the sun warm his face a little. 'I do want you to meet in person, though. I know you've chatted casually online.'

'She doesn't know you've told us all about the baby?'

'She's probably guessed. She's not talking to me right now.'

'Oh Luca. Is it really that bad, *amore mio*?'

'I don't know. She thinks I cared more about Bianca,' he said, his voice breaking with emotion.

'That woman!' his mother hissed, scorn in her voice. 'I know we have to be nice to her for Matteo's sake, but I find it hard to even look at her. This is all her fault as usual.'

'No, *Mamma*. It's mine,' he admitted. 'I should have shown Romy that I trust the woman I love.' He heard his mother's sharp intake of breath, as this was the first time she'd heard him say this about anyone other than Bianca.

'I knew it, but was waiting for you to finally tell me. I'm so sorry that you are going through this, my love. I can't wait to meet Romy in person. You need a strong woman.'

Luca smiled at this. 'I can't wait for the day you meet either. If she hasn't thrown me out of *Nonna*'s place first!' His mother chuckled at that.

'Give her time to heal. Spoil her,' she suggested. 'Show her how much you love her through your actions each and every day.'

'*Grazie, Mamma.* Love you. Speak soon,' he ended the call, after a few words about his brother Alex's equally disastrous love life. At least Alex hadn't fallen for anyone. He seemed to enjoy being single and dated widely, as Luca had before he met fiery Romy Lopez.

He heard the shower turn off and went into the kitchen to wash the dishes. Being in such a domestic setting would have appalled him a few months ago, now he craved it. He didn't care if his fancy flat lay empty. His home was wherever Romy and their child were and he'd do everything in his power to show her his true intentions. He felt the ring box he always carried in his pocket these days and an idea came to mind. He would take a leaf out of her grandparents' book and plan something special for the mother of his child. An engagement party!

Was he being too presumptuous and pushing her too far, he worried? She'd refused to be his girlfriend because he'd royally messed up, so he guessed she might not love this next idea. But he knew they loved each other, and they were already having a child together, so it was about time he asked her if she'd do him the honour of becoming his life-time partner and his wife! If she said no then he'd just have to bide his time and keep asking her until she gave in. He'd treat her like a princess, the way she deserved, and she'd never once doubt her decision to stick with the angry Italian from across the water that drove her wild with passion and angst in equal measure.

Luca grinned to himself as he started thinking of what he would need to do to make Romy realise that he meant what he said. He wasn't about to give her up, and he would do whatever it took to make her his.

Chapter 36

'You are so annoying!' Romy grumbled as Luca sat and watched her eat, but she did give him a half-smile that lifted his spirits.

'You've been working hard and you need to eat before we go out.'

Their constant sparring was wearing him down and he knew it must be hard on Romy and the baby too. Everything he did seemed to annoy her, so that he had to tiptoe around her each day. He'd tried booking her pampering sessions at the spa in town and even organised a nice lunch with her sister and grandmother, but she just said she was too busy at work. She had given in after an ear-bashing by her sister and agreed to an evening meal with her family, but she still wasn't as relaxed as he'd hoped and he hated seeing her upset. He knew she was stressing about the actual birth and whether she'd be a good mother. Reassurance that she'd be the best mother ever just made her raise a sardonic eyebrow and move away.

'Supposing I'm like my parents and want to leave my child?' she fretted.

'Romy,' Luca reassured her. 'You won't. This child will have two parents nearby, I promise you.' She sighed and let him kiss her wrist and gave him a tentative smile.

He admired the loose and flowy summer dress she was wearing that swept over her new curves. The golden colour complimented her dark brown eyes and fair hair. Her breasts looked lush and beautiful, and he tried not to stare too much as he itched to touch every part of her. He wanted to pull her into his arms whenever she wasn't grouchy with him, and even then he was tempted. She was more beautiful to him than she'd ever been, but she was also the angriest she'd ever been. She slept in his arms, but he didn't dare touch her because whatever he did, he did wrong.

'You look stunning,' he said, brushing her hair from her face and over her shoulders. Her hair was getting longer and she often wore it in a single braid down her back when she was working now, but today it was loose around her shoulders. Summer was almost over and the evenings were still warm, but he picked up a lightweight jumper for her after he checked she'd eaten something because she kept telling him she was 'hangry' recently. Apparently, that meant a combination of hungry and angry. He wanted her to be in as good a mood as possible.

He was resplendent in a tuxedo and bow tie. His shirt was crisp and white, but mightily uncomfortable because he was nervous as hell! Supposing he'd read this whole situation wrong? He hadn't exactly been the king of good decisions lately, because the woman he loved couldn't stand him a lot of the time. Usually a congenial, easy-going kind of guy, Romy thought he was irksome and in her way.

'Are you ready to go to the party?' he asked, straightening his back and getting a grip. He could do this.

'I don't know why Maya decided to have a party on the

top floor of the Mollyson Palace Hotel, of all places. It's so fancy! She usually gets caterers in at Noah's house.'

'It is her birthday,' he reasoned, pulling his shirt away from his collar so that he could breathe.

'Not until next week,' she straightened his shirt and then looked at him appreciatively. She couldn't hide that she was still attracted to him, and it gave him hope.

'Maybe she's busy then, or the hotel was booked up on that date?'

Romy heaved a huge sigh, as if it was so much trouble going to a luxurious party. He knew she was feeling insecure about her dress. There was no hiding her pregnancy now and although he adored her independence, he wished she'd let him do more than cook her an occasional dinner and rub her tired feet from time to time. The noise she made in the back of her throat when he touched her almost sent him over the edge, but he was waiting for her cue. He felt like a horny teenager with a first crush, which was ridiculous.

Luca had often had periods without sex, despite what most people around there thought of the 'Lothario Bowen brothers', but he couldn't seem to stop dreaming about making love to the woman of his dreams. Especially when she was half-naked and in the bed next to him.

'Ok. Let's get this over with... You look nice,' she added, as if she'd just noticed. His ego took another hit.

'Thanks.' He tried to keep the sarcasm out of his tone. 'I'm glad you think so.'

'You always look nice,' she admitted and he softened a little. He knew she was tired from long hours at the Wildlife Tearoom, and was worrying about where to live now Clara had deserted the bungalow. She was also probably anxious about her mooring. There weren't many good places to dock a tearoom along the river that weren't already taken. She'd been very savvy to find Clara and her berth, even though it seemed that it had all been a happy coincidence. Romy liked everyone to think that she was a daydreamer, but she was a shrewd businesswoman.

They'd had countless 'discussions' about her leaving the bungalow, but he had his own ideas about that and was firm about her staying so that he could be nearby if she needed him. His *nonna* was adamant that she wasn't coming back and was blissfully happy by the sea. He'd worried about that himself at first, but he had ideas on it too and now he was excited with the prospect of a site right opposite the Bowen boat berth. He could easily get to and from work and could keep an eye out for his family and he'd drawn up plans for Romy to look at.

She'd probably try to run away at first, but the beautiful new home he intended to build for them on the site of the bungalow would win her over. He knew she didn't need fuss or status, so he'd kept things simple, with lots of windows looking out over the water and a reading room for her to decompress after work. He'd even thought of adding a small pond for the injured ducks she treated, so they could heal, away from the bustle of the boat. They'd have to fence it in once the baby began toddling, though. The thought made a wide smile stretch onto his face and his eyes regained some sparkle. He would make this future happen because he knew Romy would love it after she got over shouting at him.

He opened the door for Romy to precede him out of the front of the bungalow, where a sleek black chauffeured car was waiting for them.

'This is a posh taxi,' she said to him under her breath,

whilst wriggling to make herself comfortable on the plush leather seats.

'I decided we both needed a night off driving,' Luca admitted. He had actually already been to the hotel earlier that day and left overnight cases that he'd packed in their room, but he wasn't telling her that yet. She might kill him!

Chapter 37

Romy had let Luca help her into the very comfortable car and tried to be excited for her sister. Maya didn't often throw ostentatious parties like this, but Romy guessed that becoming famous and dating a film star had changed her life. Maya herself hadn't changed, though. She was still the same bossy sister she'd always been, Romy smiled to herself. She adored her siblings and needed to stop being so grouchy and to smile more. Maybe Maya's tastes had altered and Romy hadn't realised? Romy herself liked hot Italian guys now and she'd never dated one before. Luca had changed everything for her and it was a big adjustment. Now she couldn't imagine what she'd seen in the very insipid Aaron.

Luca was all she could think about, beside their child, and she worried it was a tad obsessive. She knew she needed to be kinder to him, but she was scared of getting hurt and was pushing him away before he could do that again. The lies he'd told her still made her bottom lip wobble and her eyes smart with tears, which she angrily brushed away before he saw them.

She'd been staring covertly at Luca while he gazed out of the window on the journey there. He looked devilishly handsome in his dinner jacket, but she didn't want to tell him in case he got a big head. She knew she was being particularly snappy with him right now, but she didn't really know how to behave when he was near. She was constantly tearful and frustrated as hell! She was also feeling not having her mum nearby and Maya was being a bit overprotective as usual, which was lovely, but suffocating, if she was honest. Sometimes she just wanted to sit with her mum and chat about impending motherhood. It wasn't the same sitting in front of a computer when her mum could be called away any minute. It didn't exactly constitute a relaxing chat. Romy was worried about being a good mum, but felt she didn't really have much experience of one as her mum had left her behind. She refused to cry today, though, as this was her big sister's special day. She was lucky enough to have strong female role models in her sister and grandmother, as well as her mum who couldn't have worked harder to save lives, so she felt stupid being maudlin about it, when she was pretty lucky really.

'Are you ok?' Luca asked, placing his hand over hers.

'Sure,' Romy responded, not really meaning it, which made him frown.

'Let's try and enjoy ourselves tonight.'

'We will,' she tried to smile, biting her lip and watching the houses just out of town whizz by, in a blur of living room lights.

Now he knew the baby was his, Luca was faffing around her all the time and he'd stopped touching her, even though he professed to love her. Being near him was making her hormones rage and she wished he'd stop pandering and sweep her up into his arms and into bed. Instead, he was treating her as if she might break when she actually felt stronger than ever since Saffron had arrived.

The horrible thought she'd been battling was always lurking – he didn't fancy her anymore. Did her pregnant body turn him off? she wondered. Why else would he suddenly be so reticent, when he'd been all over her at first. Maybe he was bored with her, or perhaps her moods had finally driven him away. Was he staying because of the baby? All of these thoughts tumbled through her brain, and she sniffed and tried not to feel sorry for herself. She'd wanted a baby for so long, but being single and in a 'situationship' hadn't been part of the plan. She missed the steamy evenings wrapped in Luca's arms.

Romy knew she'd been giving him mixed signals, but Aaron had blown her world apart with his actions. It wasn't just Luca who had been scarred by his past. Bianca did a complete number on Luca, but what Aaron had put Romy through was just as cruel. She was still recovering from the shock. Both of them needed to decide to try and move past the hurt and build something new. It was time they each understood that their new partner was the polar opposite of their last. They needed to build trust. The problem was that it made them both vulnerable to more pain, but last night she'd decided that Luca was worth the risk. She needed to be brave and vulnerable and tell him.

His hand slid onto her knee and the usual spark of excitement fizzed on her skin. She gave him a tentative smile as the car pulled up outside a beautiful hotel. Romy took a moment to enjoy the picturesque scene before stepping out. Lights were blazing from the lobby, but it wasn't the modern glass and chrome block she'd been expecting. The building looked old but elegant, with overflowing hanging flower baskets bursting with calibrachoa, its trailing bell-shaped blooms in vibrant orange, yellow and hot pink. Deep green ivy spilt out of each wicker basket, cascading towards the floor, making the display look extravagantly sumptuous. Tall bay trees lined the walkway up to the wooden carved front door, which was propped open. Romy smiled in delight as she noted a small pond to the left of the entranceway, with an island in the centre housing a nesting shed for birds. There was a delicately crafted metal bridge over the water and a wooden gazebo that was gently lit with fairy lights around the edge. It sent light dancing across the water as the sun dipped and the sky turned inky black.

'I thought we were going to the Mollyson Palace?'

'Last minute change of plans,' he smiled.

'It's spectacular!' She gazed around at the pink and purple flowering hebe bushes that surrounded the front of the hotel, with their lush green foliage. It looked like something out of the National Trust catalogue. Inside was as much of a delight, with corniced coving and huge ornate fireplaces in the lobby and bar. Luca spoke quietly to the receptionist while Romy took in the décor, which was themed around local wildlife. She leant in to read the description under a gorgeous painting of a mallard duck. It seemed the hotel had its own history with feathered friends. As Romy turned, Luca was being handed something that he put in his pocket, which made her frown.

He led her to the lifts and she freaked out at all the mirrors. 'You look beautiful,' he said as the doors slid closed.

'Why don't you ever come near me then?' she asked huffily and his lips quirked in humour at her pout and then his eyes darkened, as this was the cue he'd been waiting for. She saw the change and backed up against the cool wall of the lift as it glided upwards to the top floor.

'Is that what you want? I was waiting for you to tell me.'

'Tell you what?'

'That you love me!' He ground out, as he pulled her rounded hips into contact with his body, his hands already at the nape of her neck and in her hair, urging her lips towards his own. Seconds later the lift doors slid open and they jumped apart, both panting and flushed, Luca's hand still cupping her hip.

'Where are we?' she asked.

'We're staying here tonight. My treat. I got us a room because of the celebration for Maya. The party is on the ground floor.'

'You got us a room?' Her skin tinged red again and she couldn't look at him for a moment, as they stepped into the hallway and he took her hand. He pulled her along the corridor, as if he couldn't wait to get inside. He held the room key up to open the door swiftly and as soon as they were inside, he kicked the door shut and backed her up against the wall with a growl.

'Luca!' she panted, her head spinning with lust as her hands slid around to feel his taut backside.

'You think I don't crave you every moment of every day?' he asked. 'It's torture!'

Her mouth hung open in shock and then she frowned. 'Then why?'

'I need to hear it,' he said fiercely and she put a hand on his chest and felt his heartbeat. 'Why won't you tell me? I know I've made mistakes, but I try to show you how much I love you every day.'

'I'm scared,' she admitted, her bottom lip trembling.

'I'm scared too, but I've never loved anyone more than I love you and I'm not letting you walk away without a fight.'

Romy gulped and felt her skin grow warmer. Aaron hadn't declared his love for her so openly, and she'd never felt this way either. What she'd had with Aaron felt childish and insipid now. She had been infatuated with her ex, nothing more. It hadn't been love.

Luca's hands were still firmly planted on her backside now and she liked it! She felt the joy of knowing he was still attracted to her. It had been on her mind so much, more than she liked to admit, and it felt good to let it go. She slid her fingers under the waistband of his suit trousers and felt warm skin. He looked like he wanted to kiss her again, but this time he kept her waiting, immobile. He was making her pay for her insolence.

'I love you,' she finally said, when he refused to let her hands wander.

Luca lifted her off her feet and swung her around in sweet joy and she laughed and told him over and over again that she loved him. Now she'd said it once it seemed natural to tell him again. When he finally put her down, after kissing her thoroughly and messing up her hair and dress, she gazed around the room in awe and tried to straighten her clothes and pretend she could concentrate on anything other than the red-hot man in front of her. She noticed that the room was bursting full of wildflowers, like the ones that grew all round the wildlife tearoom. Rose petals were strewn over the bed and a bottle of champagne was being iced in a cooler, two sparkling crystal flutes next to it. The crystal jug of orange juice next to it made Romy feel thirsty suddenly because she could smell the sharp tang of citrus mixed with the heady scent of roses and wildflowers. She could hear ducks quacking in the garden from the open windows and birds singing in nearby trees.

'What is this?' she asked in confusion.

Luca looked shifty suddenly and stepped back from her for a moment. He pulled a box out of his pocket and the bent down on one knee. Romy covered her mouth with her hand in shock and her eyes smarted with tears as he stared up at her with intent. She didn't feel scared suddenly, and elation built up and burst through, as she realised what he was about to do.

'Romy. I love you more that I can ever express, hence the wildflowers and hotel room. I know you refused to be my girlfriend, but I think we've gone beyond that now.' Romy felt like she'd been holding her breath for ages, but didn't dare let it out. 'All I want from life is for you to be my wife and for Matteo to have bundles of brothers and sisters, if that's what you want too?' Romy couldn't speak so she just sighed and nodded. 'Will you marry me?' he finally asked and she squealed and threw her arms around him, smothering him in kisses. She was fed up with arguing, even though the topics had been pretty important. She loved this man and he loved her, so why shouldn't they be happy together?

'You didn't answer me,' he held her at arms' length for a moment.

'Of course I'll marry you, Luca. I love you,' she said simply and he grabbed her around the waist and tumbled them onto the bed where he rained kisses down all over her face and neck and she squirmed in happiness. 'The party!'

'The party can wait!' he said happily as he pulled the curtains closed, rucked her dress up to her waist and stripped off the wisp of silk underwear she was wearing, throwing it to the floor. 'Luca!' she said breathlessly, but she was already reaching for his trousers and slipping them down his backside, his mouth kissing his way up her thigh.

Chapter 38

'We're an hour late!'

'It doesn't matter,' grinned Luca, pressing her wrist to his lips for a swift kiss as they walked up the corridor towards Maya's party. He held her hand and stopped her just before they went through the ornate carved double doors to the ballroom. 'Um... Romy... there's something I should explain...'

At that moment, Maya burst through the doors, seeming out of breath. Music played from inside the room and she quickly closed the doors behind her. Her dark hair was swept up with sparkly slides at each side and she was wearing one of their grandmother's latest creations, a shimmering knee-length dress in a rich red tone. The skirt swung around her legs as she moved and she was in sky-high heels.

'You look sensational!' said Romy quickly, handing her the wrapped gift she'd bought, which her sister looked at strangely before she caught herself.

'Thanks!' Maya said as she put the present down on a nearby side table and grabbed both of their hands. 'Where the hell have you been?' Then she stopped and noticed her sister's slightly dishevelled appearance and grinned. She winked at Romy who blushed and quickly smoothed her hair down with her hand. 'You're glowing, sis,' she grinned.

Romy rolled her eyes, but grinned back. 'Sorry we're late,' she mumbled. 'It's Luca's fault.'

Luca's wide smile was a bit too obvious, so Romy nudged him not so subtly. 'How's the party going?'

'Missing the guests of honour!' said Maya, clapping her hands in excitement, her eyes sparkling.

'What do you mean?' frowned Romy, looking around her for these mystery guests. Surely Maya was the girl of the moment? Maya pulled a face and mouthed sorry to Luca and slipped back behind the door before Romy could pout. 'Luca?'

'This is our engagement party...' he stilled for a moment.

'Our engagement party? What? You've only just asked me to marry you!' she squawked.

'I kind of wanted to make a big gesture and propose in front of everyone we love. I didn't know I wouldn't be able to wait that long.' He took her hand, now adorned with a diamond and white gold engagement ring, and kissed it.

'Luca!' she protested. 'I haven't had a minute to get used to the idea. The room is full of people expecting to celebrate our engagement?' she asked in horror.

'You did say yes...' he winced.

'But supposing I hadn't?'

She really wanted to know. Annoyance at his assumption flowed, but also curiosity at the predicament he'd put them both in. It was actually quite funny.

'I was prepared for it. You've rejected me before. I just hoped you'd be too embarrassed to say no.' He grinned and she couldn't help but laugh at his bravado. One of the things she loved most about him was his resilience.

'Luca!' she said for the third time and then giggled into her hand. 'You'd have embarrassed yourself to embarrass me into marrying you?' she clarified, biting her lip in mirth now. This was so ridiculous.

'I was desperate,' he admitted. 'I would do pretty much anything you needed me to, to persuade you how much I love you. I don't care how stupid I look.'

Her heart melted a little and then nerves kicked in. 'So, I got my sister that big fancy present for nothing?' she smiled.

'It is her birthday next week,' he reminded her, cupping her face in his hands and leaning in sweetly to kiss lips that were plump from his earlier kisses. 'You don't hate the idea?'

'I'm not as averse to it as I thought I would be,' she admitted and he whooped and swung her around in his arms just as Maya flung the doors open.

Romy saw hundreds of people staring back at them, broad smiles on their faces. She realised the room was full of those she loved – friends, regular customers and family. How had she suddenly amassed such an incredible group of friends, she wondered. It must have happened without her realising. She'd been so shut off from making new connections, but had been doing it anyway.

'She said yes!' Luca said loudly and everyone cheered and began surging forward to congratulate them. Romy looked around in a daze as she kissed and hugged their guests. Eventually she was led to a table at the front of the beautifully decorated room. Each table was laid with crisp white linen and colourful hand-thrown pots that were bursting with yet more wildflowers. Crystal wine glasses sparkled and she could see servers wandering round topping up everyone's glasses.

Every detail had been thought of and her heart was bursting with joy at the thoughtfulness of Luca and her family. Maya had made the invites for everyone, featuring a drawing of her Wildlife Tearoom with Bob the duck on the front. The drawing was so beautiful that Romy put a couple of the matching table settings in her bag to frame later. There were wildflowers everywhere and waiting staff wandered around with hot morsels of vegetarian food for them all to enjoy. Romy snaffled some of the tajin cauliflower bites, deep-fried olives stuffed with ricotta and guindilla chilli, and a pickled beetroot taco with goat's cheese, and placed them on the pretty vintage plate beside her. She could also see bowls of her favourite vegetable crisps with curry salt on each table. There was champagne for everyone, but sparkling alcohol-free wine for Romy and the drivers in the group, although it seemed most people were staying and the hotel was packed to the rafters.

Romy sat next to her grandmother, who was regaling everyone with stories about her husband's latest batch of fan mail. Romy's grandfather was chuckling by her side. Romy knew he was still quite stunned by the popularity of his new rare plant gardening show on television. He'd wrongly assumed no one would watch it. 'He is a bit of a dish, of course,' her grandmother was chuckling, taking Owen's hand and kissing it, just like Luca had done to Romy's earlier that evening. She sighed and hoped she and Luca were still that much in love when they retired. Then she scoffed because her grandparents were now busier than ever.

Her pops still bred exotic plants from the huge glasshouse in his garden and Ettie still cooked wonky biscuits, made incredible clothes for blockbuster films and went rollerblading on occasion. Romy leaned in as Ettie hugged her and then Luca cleared his throat at the front of the room. He was standing before a huge screen that had dropped down from the ceiling and Romy frowned. What now? Could this day get any weirder, she grinned, enjoying every moment of her mad family. Luca fitted right in, it seemed!

Clara and her date, Henry, waved from the next table and Romy blew her a kiss. Clara adored living with her 'friend' and certainly didn't intend to come back, she'd announced earlier. The question of where to live and dock her tearoom was still an ongoing problem if Clara decided to sell the bungalow, but Romy couldn't think about that now. Maybe she and Luca could put in a bid for it, she pondered thoughtfully and smiled. She had a fiancé! Who cared where they lived. She didn't, as long as they were together.

Luca pulled his collar away from his neck as his skin had a pink tinge. Romy felt for him, but it was his own fault. She wondered what he was up to. A speech, she guessed. 'I hope he doesn't expect me to stand up and give a speech too,' she whispered to her grandmother, who patted her hand in sympathy, which didn't help her nerves.

Chapter 39

Luca could feel sweat dripping down his back. He hated public speaking and wondered why he'd thought this might be a good idea. He could chat one to one, or was happy in small groups for hours, but now everyone was staring at him expectantly. Gulping some air into his lungs, he sipped his champagne to ease his suddenly dry throat as the projector sprang to life. He'd wanted Romy to understand how much he cared about her, but she'd already said yes, so now he worried this might scare her off again!

'Luca,' urged Maya kindly. 'You've got this.' Everyone was sitting at round tables dotted all over the ballroom and they were staring at him expectantly.

'Ok,' he bolstered himself. He could do this. He looked at Romy, who was smiling at him reassuringly and suddenly all his nerves melted away. This was about them and that was all that mattered. 'This feels a bit like a wedding,' he joked and everyone tittered. 'I hope you'll all come to that too.'

They all roared with laughter at this, and Romy

blanched. Luca grinned because everyone knew she'd rather get married in a field with about six people and a few ducks there. They all supported her, though, whatever her choices.

'Good luck with that!' called Romy's brother Arthur and they all laughed again.

Romy's face flamed and Luca sent her a sympathetic glance and she smiled with good humour.

'As most of you know,' Luca continued, 'Romy refused to be my girlfriend, even though I asked her about a thousand times.'

The audience chuckled and Romy blushed again.

'You're losing your touch, brother,' called Alex and Luca smiled and took the friendly barb with a roll of his eyes.

'Clearly! So, I thought I'd jump that part and try to persuade her to be my wife.'

They all *ahhed* at that.

'I booked the hotel and filled it with her favourite flowers to try and woo her,' he smiled into her eyes and she grinned a goofy smile back, her hands in her lap – her ring catching the light from the chandeliers. 'But I worried that wouldn't be enough. She is one of the most independent women I know and she doesn't need much. She certainly didn't need an annoying Italian bursting into her life and making up excuses to talk to her every day.'

He could see tears spring to Romy's eyes at that, but she was still smiling and brushed them away as her grandmother took her hand.

'It turned out that I couldn't wait to ask her to marry me, and she finally said yes!'

The whole room cheered and he waved everyone down to a hush with his hands.

'Before that, I created this short film, to try and let her know how I feel about her and our future children.' He turned to the screen and it flickered to life. 'To Romy,' he raised his glass.

Everyone in the room followed suit, chanting, 'To Romy!'

More tears sprung to Romy's eyes as she watched pictures of her tearoom from across the water. She gasped as it looked like he'd been taking photos to send to the council about the mess, but then she realised that she was in every single frame and her jaw dropped.

The photos quickly went from ones of the messy boat to the revamped Wildlife Tearoom resplendent with its bunting and takeaway service, boats stopping alongside. Luca had offered to take those shots for her flyers, but she hadn't realised he'd taken many with her in them too. She was smiling and chatting to customers and then it switched to images of her talking to Bob the duck, which made everyone laugh again and she sighed in pleasure. There was a photo of them all in their funny hats at the zoo, Matteo's face beaming at the camera, which made her heart squeeze with the emotion from that day. This was a love story. Matteo grinned from the next table, where he sat with his uncle Alex. Luca had already mentioned that Alex was looking after him that night. It wouldn't have been the same without Luca's son there.

Her eyes smarted with yet more tears and her sister nudged her so that she didn't miss anything. The next photos were of her barefoot in Clara's garden and at her grandmother's half-birthday, where Romy had been so nervous to get things right. The boat looked incredible. Then the photos scrolled through touches that made the boat special to her and her customers, including the nesting boxes, eggs, bird seed, dogs and their owners and the views from the river and garden. There were photos of her and Luca at various places where he'd insisted on selfies which she'd forgotten about, and it ended up with an image of her recent scan. Then it faded out, to applause and claps from their friends and family as they all got up to congratulate them both. Matteo hugged her, and she wrapped her arms around him for a tight squeeze.

Luca was instantly by her side. 'That was amazing,' she told him through her tears, which he brushed away gently with the pad of his thumb. His arms came protectively around her and scooped her outside for a breather away from their well-wishers. He led her onto the hedge-lined patio. It had tall poles with fairy lights strung across, and a fountain at the centre with tiny golden fish darting around a pool.

'What do you really think?' he asked, wrinkling his brow. She smoothed the lines out with her fingers and then pulled him in for a kiss that set his world alight. Would he ever get enough of this woman? He knew he wouldn't.

'I loved it. I love you. Thank you for not giving up on me,' she told him. 'A lesser man would have.'

'He'd be an idiot,' he said fiercely and she laughed, capturing his face in her hands for another quick kiss.

'I'm sorry for refusing to be your girlfriend,' she said with a grin and he swatted her bottom playfully. 'I was being stubborn, as usual. Was it worth it in the end?'

'Definitely,' he agreed.

'What about Matteo?' she asked suddenly. 'Do you think he's really ok about this?'

'He gave his consent last week,' he nodded sombrely and then winked.

'Of course he did!' she laughed. Luca had told his son

everything, to make sure he was ok with it, and this time she seemed glad.

'Bianca?'

'Not so happy, but who cares! She wasn't invited tonight. I know she's part of the family too by default, but she's not my priority. You and Matteo are.'

Romy leaned in and circled his waist with her arms, pulling him in close.

'We should plan the wedding around Matteo's school holidays, if that's ok with you?' he slipped in and she closed her eyes for a second, her shoulders bobbing up and down in mirth.

'Luca! Wedding dates already? We've literally just got engaged!'

He grinned and shrugged. 'I'm eager,' he teased.

'I noticed that!' she laughed.

He enjoyed the twinkle in her eyes. It seemed the old Romy was back, and maybe a bit of gentle sparring was going to be a healthy part of their relationship, he hoped. Especially if it ended up in the bedroom. He enjoyed swinging her over his shoulder when she was feisty and he knew she loved him taking control now and then. She would give him a waspish comeback and then wink and run, giggling and wriggling until he threw her onto the bed and their games became gasps of pleasure.

'We should go back to the party,' she nodded at the door, music filtering through as the classic Luther Vandross song, *Never Too Much*, began playing.

'Or we could sneak out and go back to our room,' he raised one cheeky eyebrow at her and she burst out laughing.

'We couldn't!'

'We could.'

'It's our engagement party,' she giggled, looking around furtively like a naughty teenager.

'So? It's our rules,' he said as he swung her up into his arms and strode back to the lift, pressing his body into hers as the lift doors slid closed. The last thing she saw was the surprised faces of her brother and sister as they caught sight of the newly engaged couple making out on their way up to their room!

Chapter 40

R omy opened the plans for the new house and scanned over them again. She couldn't believe that she'd been engaged and married within a matter of weeks, and it was now early December. Once she had agreed to marry Luca, there had been no stopping him. They'd had a quiet ceremony in Italy, with close family in an idyllic little church near where Luca was born in Bologna. The evening streets had been adorned with strings of star-shaped lights ready for Christmas, and it had felt magical as she'd walked beneath them and looked up at the inky night sky in wonder, realising that she was now Mrs Bowen.

Luca had listened when she'd said she wanted a small ceremony, but people had wandered over to slap Luca on the back and shake his hand and it had ended up as quite a party anyway. Luca's family had clearly secretly known this would happen as platter after platter of delicious food was placed on a row of tables that lined the street.

Women had come out of their houses and shaken out linen to drape over the tables and then returned with jugs full of delicately scented poinsettias in deep red and soft cream, which they placed in the centre of each table. It had brought tears to Romy's eyes because she hadn't chosen this, but it felt like a hug from the community and she'd been eternally grateful. The plates and cutlery that were brought out of each house were mismatched and added to the overall feeling of family. Luca had seemed a bit pensive until she'd given him a reassuring smile and they'd enjoyed every minute of their special day, snuggling together under blankets at the tables for warmth as the winter sun dipped lower. The hum of chatter had been soothing and Romy had completely understood why it had been so hard for Luca to leave this behind. She hoped that they could work out a way to visit regularly, even with both of their work responsibilities.

Romy had been welcomed into the family amongst hugs and kisses from everyone and Luca had been treated like returning royalty. Romy understood that a lot of the town knew about how he had suffered thanks to Bianca and they all loved him like a son, it seemed. People stopped in the street to congratulate the newlyweds. Clara had also toured the couple around and helped stop Romy from becoming overwhelmed.

It had been an exhausting whirlwind, but Romy was content and happy now that she was home with her boat and ducks. She had three staff at the tearoom and Luca had told her more about his ideas for the plot of land the bungalow stood on. Clara giving them the bungalow and berth as a wedding gift was unexpected, and Romy was still in shock.

Alex often turned up at the bungalow for dinner and her own siblings and grandparents popped in frequently. So much for a quiet life back at home. She grinned as she heard the doorbell peal and rubbed her lower back as she got up. Her belly felt ginormous now and moving around wasn't as easy as before with the baby due soon. She was becoming more used to relying on other people and she couldn't comprehend how she'd managed everything alone before.

She heard Luca answer the front door and then everything went silent, so she frowned. Her family, or Luca, usually strolled up from the promenade and came in via the back gate, so she shrugged and assumed it must be a delivery. She'd ordered so many things for her first child that the cupboards were bursting. They definitely needed more space. Glancing out of the window she checked on her tearoom. It had closed for the day and the scene was serene with the river meandering by and swans and geese milling around the boat, hopeful that some food might be dropped into the water.

She turned to see Bianca walk in with Matteo and Luca. Luca's face was ashen and Bianca's make-up was smudged and her clothes dishevelled. Romy quickly went to take Matteo's hand. She made him a mug of hot chocolate and settled him at the outside table with a cupcake and a book about river birds Luca had bought her for her birthday, which she knew Matteo loved.

She could see Luca from the kitchen, but rushed back to see what the problem was, her stomach churning. Bianca being around was never good. She was openly weeping now and Luca's stance was rigid, his eyes blazing. Romy went to his side and put her arm around his waist. 'Are you ok?'

Bianca turned to them with bleak eyes and for the first time Romy's heart went out to her. Was she sick? She looked up at Luca, but his face was set.

'Guiseppe had a doctor's appointment a few weeks ago because he wants another child.'

Romy rolled her eyes at this because of course, what Guiseppe wanted, he got. Most people tried for a child, like she had, for many years.

'They ran all kinds of tests, and today they told him he's infertile,' Bianca sobbed.

Romy's stomach dropped because she knew how it felt to be unable to have a child and the devastation that left behind. She rubbed her belly protectively and felt tears smart in the back of her eyes. She cringed when she thought about what Aaron had done to her and the invasive tests she'd endured. She immediately went to Bianca and reached out a hand in sympathy, but then stopped and frowned in confusion.

'But...but...'

'But you told me Matteo was definitely Guiseppe's!' raged Luca and Romy winced at his raised voice.

'I thought he was. I had no doubt in my mind,' Bianca's bottom lip wobbled and she flinched at the sight of Luca. 'We barely slept together by then, and I was with Guiseppe all the time.'

Luca's face hardened and Bianca flushed. Romy winced because it had only taken her one time to get pregnant with Luca too.

'You told me you'd done a paternity test,' Luca swore under his breath and began pacing. 'You showed me the letter!'

Romy knew he'd never trust another word this woman said again.

'I was going to read the results, but I was so sure! Guiseppe only wanted to marry me if I brought Matteo with me. He wasn't interested before that. So yes, I did the test... but I never opened it. I pretended I had, because I knew the results... I thought.' She pulled a sealed letter from her purse and put it on the counter top. 'Guiseppe has thrown me out.'

'I don't blame him!'

'I'm still so shocked, Luca,' Bianca said, pleading for understanding. 'I don't know how this happened. We barely saw each other at that time because you were always working.'

Romy seethed under her breath. Matteo was outside and he definitely didn't need to hear this right now.

'To try to make a living for my family,' Luca said, and Romy could see how much pain he was in and how much effort it must have taken him not to shout and scare Matteo.

'How do you know that's even yours?' she threw at him, pointing at Romy's tummy.

'Because Romy is not you, Bianca,' he said scathingly and her face flamed.

'I'm going back to Italy,' she sobbed, waiting for him to explode.

'No,' he commanded, refusing to take the bait. 'You did this. You hurt me and Matteo more than you should ever hurt someone you profess to care about. Even Guiseppe's world will now be destroyed. I know what that is like. He is going through what I went through when Matteo was four.'

Romy tried and failed to feel sympathy for Guiseppe, the man who had so ruthlessly taken Luca's son away and moved to another country with him.

Bianca continued to sob but no one went to comfort her.

'I changed my whole life to be near my son after you carelessly moved abroad, Bianca, without a thought to the pain you caused me, or Matteo. Supposing I hadn't and we had no relationship now?' Luca cried out in frustration, his voice breaking. Fresh tears sprang to Bianca's eyes and Romy sniffed and swiftly wiped her own damp eyes. 'My son!' he said finally and Romy felt a spark of light filter through the gloom.

'Guiseppe hates me,' Bianca sniffed, her shoulders bobbing up and down as she cried.

'Guiseppe is hurting,' Luca said. He had been in exactly the same situation, Romy knew.

Her empathy didn't extend to Luca's ex-wife anymore, though. This woman was a master manipulator, and the cost had been too high for the rest of them. Romy reached out and took Luca's hand in her own. She could see by the set of his shoulders how much pain he was in, but he squeezed her hand in appreciation of her support.

'Guiseppe loves you, despite your antics, Bianca,' said Luca. 'Who the hell knows why, after the way you behave. Go home. Apologise to your husband. Tell him it was an 'honest' mistake and show him you love him,' he said, disgust showing on his face. 'You do love him?' She nodded vehemently and stood up. 'Maybe he'll forgive you. I won't this time. You stole four years of my son's life from me when you moved away.'

'I'm so sorry,' Bianca turned to Romy, as if she might help her, but Romy stayed by Lucas side, her face immobile. Romy's heart broke for her husband and what this one selfish person had done to his life.

'You wouldn't have met Romy or had that baby,' Bianca said, pointing to Romy's stomach again. 'If I hadn't moved here with Guiseppe.'

Romy cringed at such insensitivity, and Luca's jaw set in anger as his eyes blazed. 'You think you are to thank for that?' Luca laughed sardonically. They both knew it had taken months of fighting and wooing to win Romy's heart. 'She's my soul mate. I would have found her, wherever she was on this earth.'

Romy gasped as her heart melted and Bianca's face drained of colour.

'Can I leave Matteo with you?' Bianca asked, rapidly changing tack as she picked up her bag and left the damning letter on the counter.

'Of course,' he answered automatically and then swung around to look at Romy, who nodded her assent, even though the fire was back in her eyes too.

How dare this woman think the whole world revolved around her and her emotions. What about the young boy who was currently sitting outside, confused about why his mother was crying and why both sets of his parents were arguing.

She could see Luca had the same thought. His protective instincts were already in place for Matteo. Although she hadn't thought she could love this man more, she did now in this instant. Thanks to Bianca, his world was shattering again, but he was staying relatively calm for the sake of his son, when she knew his insides would be raging like the fires of hell.

He didn't need to ask her if his son could stay and he could see she was horrified by what Bianca had said. Romy closed the door after his ex-wife left and turned to the love of her life. Matteo ran into Luca's arms when he heard the door shut and Luca hugged him to his side as he opened his other arm for Romy to join them. Fresh tears sprang to all their eyes, but then they looked at each other and offered up wonky smiles. Was it wrong to feel so elated and so angry at the same time?

'Matteo,' Luca said gently, ruffling the top of his son's hair, as he stepped back. 'I'm sorry for all you've been though – what we've all been through. Do you want to talk about it? Has Mum explained what has happened?'

'Not really,' Matteo replied, while nibbling on his lower lip. 'She just said you are my real dad and she made a mistake. I'm confused. I know we live with Guiseppe, but I always thought you were my real dad,' his mouth set into a firm stubborn line, which mirrored his father's.

Romy smiled, finally, and Luca chuckled, some tension dissipating from the air. When Luca took Matteo to sit on the couch, the boy's face looked so like her husband's that Romy wondered how they hadn't questioned things before. Bianca had hoodwinked them all for her own gain – yet again, it seemed.

'He wasn't horrible to me and he bought me lots of toys, but I didn't want to call him Dad, even though I had too,' Matteo added, mutiny in his tone. 'I thought of him as my stepdad anyway. I always knew you were my real dad, just like you said you were. I grew up with you,' he added simply, as if that resolved everything. *Out of the mouth of babes*, thought Romy. If only things really were that simple.

Romy laughed and Luca's lips quirked up, even though she could tell he was exhausted. 'So much like your father,' she joked, nudging Luca's leg until he finally raised a real smile. 'Stubbornness is in the Bowen genes,' she grinned.

'So, you're ok with me being your biological father?' Luca needed to know and Romy took his hand a gave it a squeeze of support.

Matteo shrugged and then smiled when his dad hugged him again. 'You've always been my proper dad,' he sighed, snuggling into the hug.

Luca's shoulders relaxed and so did Romy's. She rubbed her belly and looked at her family. Their child was going to have an amazing big brother.

Romy glanced at Luca for his assent and got the latest scan out of a drawer. 'How do you feel about being a big brother to a little sister?' Matteo's eyes went wide and then a huge grin spread across his face.

'A sister?'

'We decided to find out because I kept painting the walls different colours and your dad was impatient as always,' she teased. She noticed Luca hadn't let go of his son, and she didn't blame him. What this meant for them all, she didn't know, but she was sure no one would ever be able to take Luca's son away from him again. The pain might just be worth it for that.

Matteo jumped up and asked if he could go and play in the garden with the ducks, as Bob had just waddled up from the path. Luca didn't look like he wanted to let his son out of his sight, but she put a hand on his arm as they watched Matteo go. She filled the cafetiere to make him a strong coffee and placed the letter Bianca had left in front of him, pulling a second, similar-looking letter out of a kitchen drawer. Both were sealed.

'I think it's time for you to look at these. I didn't open mine either, because there was only you, but you deserve never to doubt the truth again.'

Luca nodded and solemnly opened first Bianca's and then Romy's paternity tests. He laid them out on the table before him and put his head in his hands, as the results were the same.

'I should have asked to see inside Bianca's letter. I saw she had it and didn't notice it was sealed because she just showed me the front and waved it around in my face,' he said, exhaustion seeping into his voice.

'You checked the paternity test had been done. You told me,' Romy reassured him. 'Why would you ever think she would lie about the results? She knew it would crucify you.'

'She should have opened the letter.'

'I didn't open mine,' Romy reasoned.

'You didn't need to,' he sighed, rubbing his neck.

She moved closer and massaged his shoulders for a moment, until the rigidity eased.

'She wanted Guiseppe to be Matteo's father and clearly thought that was the way to win him back. She either absolutely thought Matteo had to be his, so there was no point opening the letter, or she didn't want to risk knowing in case the lie caught up with her. This way she had a get-out clause, because she could attest it was an innocent mistake. Either way, it's pretty twisted,' Romy said, hoisting herself onto one of the new kitchen bar stools they had bought, but then regretting her idea as her stomach was feeling decidedly heavy, and a bit sore if she was honest. 'I'm so sorry she put you through this.'

'You too,' he pointed out. 'You didn't sign up for this when you met me.'

'I signed up for a sexy Italian single father, and that's what I got,' she nudged his shoulder as he'd come to sit next to her. He finally smiled, then she gasped as a pain shot all around her stomach and back.

'Romy?' Luca frowned, immediately on alert as she heaved herself off the stool, winced and doubled over.

Luca jumped to help her, but she let out a groan of pain. She was a vet and had helped countless animals give birth, but the start of her own labour stopped her in her tracks. The baby wasn't due for another couple of weeks and her parents had always talked about how each of their children had been born past their due dates. She'd been hoping for a relaxed first Christmas as a married woman, with her husband, as she was actually becoming quite anxious about the birth and was putting off thinking about it too much. Romy raised panicked eyes to Luca as another wall of pain hit her and she started puffing out her cheeks to try and calm her nerves and sat gingerly down on the couch.

'Maybe it's a false alarm?' she hedged as Luca picked up the phone to ask someone to come and look after Matteo.

'We can't leave him, after the news he's just found out,' said Romy, her pulse picking up with mild panic. 'Grab my hospital bag and some books and electronic games for Matteo and we can call Maya to come and sit with him there.'

'You sure?' Luca didn't seem convinced.

'I'm sure. He'll want to meet his sister as soon as she's here and I don't want him to feel worried or shut out.'

Luca's face broke into a smile at last and he captured her face and kissed her lips softly, just as another contraction resonated around her and made her catch her breath.

'Your contractions aren't that far apart...' Luca worried.

'I'd noticed...' she parried, trying to stay calm. 'Luca – get the car!' she urged.

Luca jumped up and scrambled around, throwing things into a pile by the door and then bundling them all into his car. He called to his son and gently led Romy to the car and eased her into the front seat, moving the chair back to give her extra room. Starting the engine, he handed his phone to a rather stunned Matteo and asked him to call Maya to alert the rest of the family.

Chapter 41

'W as it the shock of Bianca's news that started your labour?' asked Maya as she fussed around her sister and checked on peacefully slumbering baby Bella in the cot beside her chair at the bungalow. 'I can't believe she had the cheek to turn up at your house and then leave Matteo there after dropping that bombshell.'

Maya's temper had eased now the baby was here, but Romy understood her protective instincts around Luca and Matteo. They were part of Romy's family now and would be protected as such. Maya was already enjoying her aunt duties and she and Matteo got on famously – especially because she often let him swim in her pool beside the river.

Romy wondered when she was going to find the time to finish her Christmas shopping, with a tiny baby in tow. As it was, she'd had to leave her staff running the Wildlife Tearoom and trust them with the responsibility. The place was thriving, and both staff and customers often popped by the bungalow to offer congratulations. Romy had swaddled Bella warmly and taken her for a stroll along the river, stopping for a coffee and a chat on the way back, much to her husband's amusement. 'You can't keep away from the place,' he'd teased, even though he was already back at work on his own boats. He did seem to take an inordinate number of breaks though, Romy sniggered, enjoying every moment of it.

'Bianca is a law unto herself,' answered Romy, gazing lovingly down at her child, who already had a shock of black hair on her beautiful head. Maya's eyes sparkled as she fussed around and tidied up the kitchen, which Romy was eternally grateful for. How could one tiny human create so much mess? They had drawers overflowing with wipes, bibs, nappies and other baby paraphernalia.

Obsessively clean Maya was staying so calm in the face of a messy kitchen. Romy didn't know how she was managing it, but she appreciated her effort. It felt great to be surrounded by people she loved. She was astounded by how protective she was over her daughter and Matteo, who was as obsessed by his sister as they all were. Romy couldn't quite take in that someone so perfect could be part of their lives.

'I can't believe Bianca has flown to the Maldives with Guiseppe for a make-or-break holiday,' said Maya. 'Leaving Matteo with you over Christmas, of course,' she seethed. 'Not that he isn't a complete angel.'

'He has his moments,' grinned Romy. 'I'm glad he's with us for Christmas and we can celebrate with you all. We can forget about Bianca for now.'

'She has such a cheek, calling me first to talk over her plans with Guiseppe, because you were inconveniently in labour and Luca was with you.' Maya shook her head in exasperation. 'I was quite busy at that point looking after her son, too! She explained in great detail how important it was for everyone 'in the family' that she reconciled with Guiseppe.' Maya's eyes met Romy's and she rolled them in disgust.

Romy had never come across anyone like Bianca before, but sadly Maya had dealt with a similar situation when she was getting to know her boyfriend Noah, who had a very toxic ex called Tabitha. Tabitha had spread all kinds of nasty rumours about Noah and almost succeeded in splitting up Maya and her dream guy.

Romy couldn't help but see the humour in the situation, now that she was back at home with her family. Bianca would always surprise them with her inability to put others first, because each time they thought she couldn't do anything worse – she did. It was incomprehensible.

'I don't know how you can even look at that woman,' Maya grumbled, but then her face lit up when her niece opened her eyes and then her eyelashes fluttered and she dropped back to sleep.

'She smiled at me!' Maya moved nearer to Romy and gave her a hug, which made her wince a little, as movement wasn't too comfortable yet.

Romy didn't have the heart to tell her sister that it was probably wind or an involuntary reflex, as newborns often took around six to eight weeks to smile in response to a social situation. Romy had read every book she could find on parenting and newborns, and she still didn't feel like she knew what the hell she was doing most days. She was grateful to have her family near, or she might have felt a bit useless and lost.

Luca had called his family after Bella had been born and Maya had informed their mum and dad, who had promised to visit soon. In fact, both sets of parents would probably arrive around the same time, so they would be able to meet up again.

Maya picked up a framed photo of Romy, Matteo and Luca on their wedding day and smiled. 'Mum and Dad got on well with Luca's parents,' she said, and Romy nodded. 'The two families seem to mesh seamlessly. It's no wonder that you loved Clara first and then her grandson. You were clearly meant to be part of their family too.'

Romy smiled at this and she took the photo from her sister and gazed at her own beaming face.

'You would never have guessed you could be so happy, when you spent most of last year scowling at Luca,' Maya joked.

Romy poked her tongue out at her. Her family was huge now but instead of feeling overwhelmed, contentment filled her veins.

Ettie and Owen had arrived within the hour of Bella's birth, arms full of delicious vegetarian nibbles and deeply scented red roses, snipped from her grandad's garden, which had made Romy's heart swell. It had felt wonderful to be surrounded by people she loved. For the first time in as long as she remembered, she was happy to rely on them all to rally around her and Luca, and help them figure this whole Bianca mess out.

Romy had fallen in love with Matteo the first time she met him, and would protect him until the day she died. Not that he needed that with a dad like Luca, she smiled to herself. Luca was strutting around like a proud peacock. He'd taken Bella and introduced her to all of his staff.

Matteo was just as proud of his baby sister and followed them everywhere. Romy suspected he was worried his dad might be taken from him again. He was slightly clingy right now, which was to be understood, but he was equally besotted with his sister. Bella had grabbed his fingers and batted her thick sooty lashes at him and Matteo had even introduced her to Bob the duck, which had made Romy chuckle. Bob hadn't seemed that interested and had turned his tail and wandered back to the boat.

'Matteo will be living here with us from now on,' said Romy, enjoying surprising her sister. 'Bianca wants to be with Guiseppe all the time, in the hope he will eventually forgive her, and his job has just changed, which means more travelling. That isn't fair for Matteo. She's covering all bases.'

'She'll still see Matteo, though?' Maya asked.

Romy nodded. 'Unfortunately,' she sighed. 'Well, I don't mean that of course, but she is exhausting! Everything is about her. She even turned my labour into a fiasco with constant phone calls about her wellbeing – not mine!'

Romy had to laugh because it was so Bianca, and she was kind of used to that now. 'Matteo loves her, as he should, and we'll work something out. She's not moving in, though!' she joked with a shudder.

'Show me the plans for your new home,' grinned Maya, deftly changing the subject. Romy handed her the drawings and they spent the next twenty minutes going over the extensions and new rooms for Matteo and Bella as she grew.

'How's things with you and Noah?' Romy asked and Maya's eyes lit up.

'He's asked me to marry him,' Maya said, clearly enjoying surprising her sibling as much as Romy did.

Romy squeaked with joy and jumped up, hugging her sister close, which made Bella wake up. Romy reached for her and settled her into her arms, cooing to her baby and rocking her back to sleep, knowing she would wake up fully for a feed soon.

'Congratulations, Maya.'

Romy couldn't have been happier for her sister, who was definitely in love with her handsome movie star. She was hoping her brother Arthur would add to his family soon. He lived with Daisy and her daughter Brontë, and he was getting broody, especially now that Romy had a baby. He kept popping round and asking to hold his niece, and they looked the picture of tranquillity together. Not bad for a relationship-averse guy!

Bella woke up with all the laughing and hugging, and let out a small cry for milk. Romy kissed her soft cheek, cuddling her to her chest for a moment and inhaling her sweet powdery baby scent.

Luca came in from work with Matteo at his side and he grinned when he saw his wife and child. Matteo ran over to kiss his sister and Romy enjoyed the way Bella got so excited to see her brother after he'd been at his new school, then helped his dad on the boats before coming home. Romy even wondered if Matteo and Bella would one day run the Bowen boats, her tearoom, or something else completely.

She couldn't believe how much her life had changed, from solitary days with nothing but resentment and anger, to a home full of people she loved and two thriving businesses.

'Maya is getting married!' she called out to everyone and Maya flushed, but accepted congratulatory hugs. 'All we need to do now is find someone who will put up with your brother Alex,' Romy joked to Luca.

They all loved Alex, but he enjoyed the single life too much to ever settle down. Romy had an inkling there was a certain lady he did have his eye on, but it seemed she didn't want anything serious. Usually that would suit Alex, but he'd grumbled about it lately when he and Romy were alone. She was his best friend's sister, so perhaps that was getting in the way, Romy wondered? She could see the cogs of Luca's brain whirring as he ran through the hundreds of possibilities who might tame his brother, and dismissed them all. He shook his head and grinned as he took his daughter and crooned softly to her as he rocked her gently while Romy prepared to give her some milk.

'I do have five brothers, you know?' his eyes sparkled and then she saw fear slide into them as she took on the challenge to find them all a girlfriend, or wife. 'There's no way you'll get any of them to settle down.'

'That's what they said about you,' Maya grinned.

Luca bent in and kissed Romy sweetly on the lips, but she knew he would keep more sizzling ones for her later and her blood warmed up as his fingers trailed along her arm for a few seconds and their eyes met with a secret smile.

'Best decision I ever made,' he grinned as he handed his sleepy daughter back to his wife and ruffled his son's hair, making them both smile. 'Happy wife, blissful life.'

Acknowledgments

A big thank you, to you, my wonderful readers. If you have read this book as the third in the series, you'll know the characters well by now. I hope you love them as much as I do. If you have read it as a standalone, then more adventure awaits with books one and two!

I adore writing romance and hope my stories make you smile and also encourage you to relax for a while between the pages. The reading and writing communities are such wonderful places to meet people who loves books as much as we do.

Thanks to my incredible ARC and street team, including advance readers, Meena Kumari, Susan Buchanan, Rie Allen Linton, Lyndsey King, Ritu Kaur BP, Donna Siggers, Cora Ryan and Claire Rowlands. You keep me writing and offer invaluable advice and support. A big shout out to my writing girls, Carrie Elks, Lorna Cook, Emma Robinson, Lizzie Page, Julie Haworth, Susan Buchanan, Glynis Peters and Chris Penhall. I love our creative chats and appreciate your guidance. Huge thanks to Sue Baker and the members of Riveting Reads & Vintage Vibes book club for hosting my online book launches and for always sharing news about my books and launches far and wide. Book clubs are amazing places to meet new friends.

I appreciate you all for picking up my books, for telling

your friends and for the brilliant reviews you write and share. From Lizzie. X

About the Author

International bestselling author and award-winning inventor, Lizzie Chantree has been featured on television and radio. She discovered her love of writing fiction when her children were little. She now writes books full of friendship and laughter, that are about women who are far stronger than they realise. She lives with her family on the coast in Essex. Visit her website at www.lizziechantree.com or follow her on X @Lizzie_Chantree

Sign up to Lizzie's newsletter for a FREE pdf book tracker where you can record your favourite reads, book boyfriends, reviews, characters, wish list, swoon rating and more. Plus a monthly monthly prize giveaway! www. lizziechantree.com

If you liked reading my novel, please consider leaving a review. Many readers look to the reviews first when deciding which book to choose, and seeing your review might help them discover this one. I appreciate your help and support. Make an author smile today. Leave a review! Thank you so much. From Lizzie :)

facebook.com/lizziechantree

x.com/Lizzie_Chantree

instagram.com/lizzie_chantree

Praise for Lizzie Chantree

'An absolute page turner, full of romance that will make you swoon. A 5 star read. I now want to visit Windsor.'

'The start of another enchanting series! I'm now getting impatient to read the next one!'

'I LOVE, LOVE, LOVE this!'

'Romance at its best!'

'I would recommend this book to anyone.'

'My recommendation: Get a copy!'

'This book has spice, lost love, new beginnings and a beautiful storyline. I can't wait for the next book!'

'Wow what a stunning story! A beautiful setting. It was perfectly described and it has made me long to visit wonderful Windsor. Can't wait to return for the next book in the series!'

'I absolutely loved this, fake dating, modern day fairytale with a strong female lead twist! Roll on for The Windsor Love Connection .....'

'Dive into this fun, romance filled with art, drama, design and diamonds, as well as devoted family and friends. The swamp girl made me laugh. Recommended summer must read for romance fans.'

'Lizzie Chantree writes lovely romance novels and her latest is no exception. Her strengths lie in creating wonderful characters, beguiling settings and simple but effective story lines.'

'Couldn't put it down.'

'A great bit of escapism!'

'I would happily devour a second sitting.'

'I was enthralled by this beautiful book.'

The Little Ice Cream Shop By The Sea

Enemies to lovers, small town love!

Chapter 1

Not *again!* Genie Grayson wanted to scream and throw her hands in the air. Instead, she stuffed her fist in her mouth and turned away. She'd thought she had her terrible phobia under control – she was a perfectly sane twenty-two-year-old – but the last few weeks had been stressful, and this was her Achilles heel. She looked around furtively to see if anyone had noticed, but there was hardly anyone enjoying breakfast in her family's seafront restaurant.

The evil seagull had dropped a lump of cheese onto her pristine outdoor tablecloth. After flying right into the restaurant awning. It had obviously been at the beer that always ended up in the gutters after a busy night at one of the clubs further down the beach.

Genie rarely admitted to having this issue, as who in the world, other than herself of course, had a problem with cheese? No one who managed a restaurant and ice cream parlour, that was for sure. Not a responsible professional who served food all day and had to be surrounded by the awful stretchy stuff that smelt like her grandad's old socks after a day on his feet.

She knew if she recited the alphabet backwards she'd be ok. She'd had years of practice. She usually got to about W, and then her pulse slowed down and she was able to take a deep breath and move on. She looked up and saw the gull sitting on the wall above the restaurant, its piercing red eyes like lasers. She shushed it away, but it just turned its back on her.

She often wondered if she had an allergy to wild animals. She'd tried to pet one at a zoo on a school trip and got bitten, then her hand had swollen up and she'd been rushed to hospital, even though she'd been fine after a few hours. She'd avoided zoos ever since. She gave the jungle a wide berth too. It wasn't too difficult from her current location on the coast of Essex, but she wasn't taking any chances. Cheese, on the other hand, was impossible to dodge. Not only did she work in kitchens, she cooked when her dad had a day off. Luckily, their bestsellers were their huge breakfasts, and plates of fish and chips.

Genie knew that if she gave into the urge to shove the offending messy table into the road, she'd get herself in all kinds of trouble with her parents, and probably the local council. She was already on their radar for changing all the restaurant's lightbulbs to a deep shade of red one weekend, to create an ambience. She'd had a formal letter the following week suggesting she might be moonlighting as a sex worker. That was slander! She might be a bit busty, and she was down on her luck, but she was too tired to blink some days. She just plastered on a smile and worked through it. Takings really had to pick up, at the restaurant though. They needed more customers.

She had to find a way to calm down and reasonably

work out a plan of action, either by talking to her mum, Milly, about their current dilemma, or by finding a boyfriend and having some hot steamy sex to take her mind off things. While she pondered that thought, she grabbed the tablecloth by the edges with a couple of forks and shoved it behind the counter into the washing basket, quickly re-covering the table with a fresh cloth.

Genie smiled brightly at two school mums who were perusing the menu but her grin dropped as she turned towards the kitchen at the back of the little restaurant. She wondered if anyone would notice if she stood in the middle of the room and screamed. Probably not.

The mums were the only two customers, and they'd already caught her cursing in Spanish under her breath as she wiped down the tables when they'd arrived. They had looked at her in confusion. She'd picked up a 'learn to speak Spanish' course at the charity shop the week previously, in the hope that she might one day travel abroad with friends. She'd also thought it might help if they ever got a foreign customer, however unlikely that seemed. But when she'd got the disc back to the house, it was a homemade knock-off copy and the only vocabulary was swearwords. She hated being conned, so she'd resolutely learned the whole tape, which consisted of about fifty phrases that all sounded mightily dodgy. They were great for easing frustration, though, as no one else knew what she was saying. She hoped. She'd looked up a few of the words, but then been worried her parents would question why she was Google-translating so many profanities. She didn't want them to start to wonder if that council letter had been spot on.

Usually, the breathtaking panorama of sandy beaches and the endless skyline across the road were enough to lift her spirits. But today she felt she might as well go and bang her head against a wall, instead of trying yet again to reason with her parents. The family business *had* to be brought into the twenty-first century. She knew she had a temper and didn't always explain things clearly without combusting into flames, but they still treated her as if she was nine years old.

All she was asking of her parents was that they let her try out a few new business ideas and a handful of new ice-cream flavours. She didn't want to reinvent the wheel. Their business hadn't changed for decades. They still had the same chairs and tables, and even the menus, that her grandad Gus had installed. Her parents' restaurant, Graysons', offered bought-in, basic puddings, but Genie had seen massive growth in big gooey ice cream desserts presented in glass mugs or tall glasses. She didn't see why they couldn't try this. They had a prime site on the seafront, for goodness sake! She could feel her temper begin to rise again. Then she remembered – their customers. She didn't want to scare them away. She twirled round to face them again with another smile.

Her parents were worried about upsetting her grandad, who ran the ice cream bar. He only offered about six flavours these days. She had spent much of her time with him and her grandma when she was growing up. Her parents had stepped in to take over the business when her grandma had died a few years previously. Her grandad had begun wandering around the small garden at the back of the restaurant and shouting at the plants, raging at the loss of his wife. In the end, they'd explained to customers that he was an inventor seeing if upsetting plants stunted their growth. It was the only explanation they could come up with for his behaviour, which was becoming more and more erratic.

Their regulars knew about Genie's grandma and understood Gus's sorrow and anger, but occasionally a new customer would start to glance around to see if there were spaces to eat elsewhere, which meant even less income for them all. Genie missed her grandma Vera terribly, as she had always let her sit with them after school. Genie would perch on a high stool behind the ice cream counter and Vera would tempt her with her latest ice cream concoction and cuddle her, while Gus served a steady stream of customers anxious to get Vera's new flavours before they sold out.

With Genie's parents selling breakfasts and lunches, and Gus and Vera on ice cream, the restaurant had worked like a dream. Then her grandma died and Genie's parents had taken the reins, working harder than ever to cover their grief. They looked more frazzled as each year passed. Genie was used to coming home from school to the empty house they lived in, up the hill, as her parents were always working. Soon, she was roped into doing her homework at the restaurant, and then it seemed a natural progression for her to help out. She'd been doing that since she could walk anyway. She loved the restaurant and was proud of her family's heritage. She needed to spread her creative wings, though, and felt that since Vera had passed away, Gus was wilting. She wanted to keep her grandma's spirit alive, and Gus needed Genie more than her parents did right now.

She spent her weekend evenings making batches of ice cream for him to sell, though he kept telling her she should be out partying with people her own age, not keeping an old man company and trying to keep his business alive. He was bored one night and bought two whippy-type machines for simple, smooth ice cream and declared that she wouldn't need to help him anymore. It broke her heart. She could see that he was trying really hard to manage alone, but he was struggling with his memories of his beautiful wife and the happiness she'd given everyone with her smile and her amazing ice cream flavours. He just couldn't replicate them.

Genie had asked him about trying different recipes, but he'd harrumphed and told her that if she thought she knew better, then she could get on with it. And besides, he'd added that there wasn't enough business to try new ideas. He liked his whippy ice cream machines and they did sell a fair amount of cones, but there was no love in the ingredients. Vera used to sprinkle chocolate chips, lemon rind, tiny bites of apple and many other incredible ingredients into her mixes to make you feel like you were eating a mouthful of magic. Your tongue would tingle and most people came back to order more. People visited from miles around to try her latest flavours. Recently Genie had decided to try to keep the tradition going. After five generations of her family running this business, she was determined to make it shine again, in honour of her grandma.

As far as she was concerned, Gus had given her the green light. She'd always worked hard for her parents and was determined to turn their fortunes round. All the shops along the seafront were looking a bit tired these days. She felt they'd get stuck in a time warp if something didn't change.

She tried to calm herself down. She chanted a mantra in her head that she'd heard on the radio that morning. It was supposed to make you feel zen, but it soon irritated her now she couldn't get the stupid phrases out of her mind.

Her parents had often told Genie she was too bossy for her own good, but then, she'd had to be. Her schoolwork had suffered and she'd failed most of her exams, because she was always helping out at the restaurant or washing and cleaning at home while her parents were at work. Her parents had despaired, but what else could they have expected?

It was why she hadn't yet found a home of her own, even at her age. Her parents had moved into her grandparents' Georgian seafront property when Genie had been just two. The house and the business were their lives. She secretly couldn't imagine living anywhere else, but she'd never tell her mum and dad that. Her grandad had moved into the annex, which was separate from the main house. He'd recently paid a man to put a fence up between the two buildings, saying he needed more privacy. Genie suspected that he wanted to be able to hide away with his grief. She felt that she couldn't express her own sorrow, as she had to keep everyone else's spirits up. Her dad walked around looking permanently grumpy and her mum often wrung her hands, which in turn made Genie anxious. Genie did the restaurant books, so she knew that they could just about scrape by for now, but how long that would last for, she had no idea. They needed something to change – and fast.

Maintaining the house, her family and the restaurant was a full time job. Although none of the whole parade of restaurants were up to date, they were still quite busy as very few bars and eateries were allowed on each stretch of beach. They rarely came up for sale, tending to stay within a family. Everybody was friends with everyone else, but the décor in each venue was old fashioned, as far as Genie was concerned, and their clientele was getting older too.

That was fine, Genie respected older people, but a few tended to sit for hours, hogging the tables, and they didn't spend much money. She'd almost poked an elderly man's eye out once when she'd thought he might be dead and was checking he was still breathing. Thank goodness, he'd woken up with a start. As an only child, she loved it when there was a mix of ages mingling around. Her dad was an only child too, so there were no siblings to help him run the restaurant. It had fallen to Genie and her mum. But since Vera had died, it felt like the life and soul of the place had gone with her.

The school mums, who were regulars and probably their youngest customers, checked their designer watches to see how much time they could spend relaxing before rushing off to pick up various offspring. It was still only 9.30am, so she wandered over to take their order and chatted amiably, as she did with all their customers, biting back her frustration.

It was hard keeping up a cheerful face with the customers, when she knew that the restaurant's takings were down again that quarter. The quiet worry that seemed to be with her most days was starting to make itself more apparent. Even if it meant more of her mum's death stares, or her dad's rolling eyes, she was determined to turn the family's fortunes around.

Continue reading here!
viewbook.at/IceCreamShopByTheSea

Also by Lizzie Chantree

Romantic Fiction

The Windsor Riverside Romance Series

Book 1

The Windsor Love Pact

Book 2

The Windsor Love Connection

Book 3

The Windsor Love Match

The Little Shop By The Sea Series

Book 1

The Little Ice Cream Shop By The Sea

Book 2

The Little Cupcake Shop By The Sea

The Cherry Blossom Lane Series

Book 1

My Perfect Ex

Book 2

The One That He Wants

Book 3

The Eternal Bachelor

<u>If You Love Me, I'm Yours</u>

The Woman Who Felt Invisible

Ninja School Mum

Babe Driven

Love's Child

Finding Gina

Non-Fiction

Networking For Writers

www.ingramcontent.com/pod-product-compliance
Lightning Source LLC
Chambersburg PA
CBHW060420180626
46817CB00007B/2600